GHOST BUSTING MYSTERY

SHADY HOOSIER DETECTIVE AGENCY SERIES

BOOK 1

DAISY PETTLES

The *Ghost Busting Mystery* (*Shady Hoosier Detective Agency Series, Book One*) is a work of fiction. All references to people, locations, and events are understood as a part of the fictive process. All characters and events in this crime comedy book series are the product of the author's imagination. Nothing in this novel is real, other than the great state of Indiana.

First Print and ebook Editions: November 2018

Hot Pants Press, LLC
Underhill, VT 05489

Book layout by www.ebooklaunch.com

ISBN: 978-0-9815678-2-2 (Print)
ISBN: 978-0-9815678-3-9 (Ebook)

Website: https://www.DaisyPettles.com

Email: daisy@daisypettles.com

Facebook: https://www.facebook.com/daisy.pettles.author

Twitter: @DaisyPettles

Chapter One

D ode Schneider wasn't right in the head even before that snowplow hit him. That was probably why no one paid him much mind when he started rattling on about ghosts. "They are hanging in the apple orchard, over at the Wyatt mansion, right regular."

"What are they doing?" asked Boots Gibson, Pawpaw County's sheriff.

"Well, gosh darn, if I knew that, I wouldn't be here jawing at you."

It was late Spring, but Dode, a bachelor farmer, was dressed in a long-sleeved plaid flannel shirt buttoned in a choke hold around his scrawny neck. Tiny dots of white tissue paper stuck to his chin where he'd nicked himself shaving. His eyes were moist, runny with pollen. He pulled a red handkerchief out of the pocket of his bibbed overalls and dabbed at his nose before honking into it. "You gonna do your job, or what?" he asked Boots.

"For crying out loud, Dode, that mansion is abandoned," said Boots. "The Wyatts all died off years ago. Place is falling down. No one goes there no more."

"Well, I know that. The way I see it," Dode leaned forward, "them ghosts are trespassing. Can't you arrest them for that?"

Boots stretched out in his chair and planted the heels of his cowboy boots firmly on the lip of his desk. He crossed both arms across his chest. He looked like a flustered Santa Claus in blue jeans. His white beard was neatly trimmed. His face was bright red, partly from farming on the weekends, but mostly from trying to reason with Dode.

We were all sitting together in the sheriff's office: Dode Schneider, Boots Gibson, and me. My name is Ruby Jane Waskom—RJ to most—and I'm a sixty-seven-year-old, detective-in-training with the Harry Shades Private Detective Agency, the best—okay the *only*—PI agency in Knobby Waters, Indiana. Knobby Waters is a small town, big enough to make it onto the map, but small enough that it is barely a pimple of a speed bump in the asphalt on State Road 235. We don't get much excitement, so I, for one, was eager to hear more of Dode's ghost story.

Boots, on the other hand, had been trying all week to dissuade Dode from filing a formal police complaint against the ghosts. He didn't like paperwork. What he liked was fishing down at the catfish honey hole off Greasy Creek, and Dode was seriously eating into his fishing time. The old geezer was determined to see his tax dollars in action. Boots had called me in to calm Dode down and take charge of the case.

Dode wrinkled his nose. "I'm telling you, them ghosts are up to something. Somebody ought to do something before they bust into town. Start pestering the whole lot of us."

I was trying to keep an open mind. Living people could be pretty annoying. Why should the dead be any different?

"On second thought," Dode leaned forward, whispering like he feared someone might be listening, "maybe it ain't ghosts. Maybe it's aliens. How's a fella to tell the difference?"

I thought that was a darn good question.

"Like I told you Dode, this here seems like a job for a private agency," Boots announced as he leaned back in his swivel chair. "I represent Pawpaw County. We don't do ghost busting. We police the living, not the dead. If you're being pestered by dead people, you're on your own. Your tax dollars don't cover that."

"What about if it's aliens?"

"Dang blast it, Dode. My jurisdiction doesn't extend into outer space either. Aliens would be federal, FBI."

I leaned over and whispered in Boots's ear. "You're just tired of dealing with the old coot."

"That too," he grunted.

Dode's eyes slid back and forth, taking in both of us. "You're in on it. The both of you. Ain't ya?"

"In on what?" I asked.

"The conspiracy."

Boots snorted. "The conspiracy? What in the Sam Hill?"

I cleared my throat. "Who you think is conspiring to do what, Dode?"

Dode's eyes spun. "You trying to confuse me, missy?"

"Nope. You said there was a conspiracy. What are the ghosts conspiring to do?"

"I dunno. That's why I'm sitting here consulting with the law. I want you all to find out. I just think them ghosts are up to no good. I can feel it in my bones. My busted hip has been acting up. I can divine things in my bones, you know. It's a gift I got from my mother's people."

I wanted to say it was more likely a gift of that head-on collision he'd had with the county snowplow, but I was trying to be professional.

Boots bit his bottom lip. "These ghosts, are they making any noise? Disturbing the peace? Coming onto your land?"

"No. They ain't unruly ghosts. But they are odd; not normal ghosts, you might say. They have big lights on their butts. They look like giant fireflies swinging their butts under the apple trees." Dode held out his gnarled hands. He threw them wide apart. "Really big lightning bugs."

He was so excited I thought his eyes were going to pop out of his head. Clearly, he was seeing something, and it had him riled up.

3

Boots picked up the police report. He rattled it. "Ghosts with big lighted butts? Do you hear yourself, Dode? Do you? Cause if you heard yourself, you'd be hearing a crazy man. I can't file this. You, me, the whole county, we'd be a laughing stock."

Dode chewed one little fingernail, and then the other. He'd come all the way into town to file a police report, and clearly, he wasn't giving up. "What if it's aliens, not ghosts? Everybody would want to know. Right? I mean, aliens could vaporize the world. Puff! No one wants to be puffed out of existence, now do they, eh?"

Boots shoved back from his desk. He strutted out of the office. "All yours, Ruby Jane," he spat over his shoulder as he headed toward the coffee room. "I got some real policing to do."

"The sheriff can't help you, Dode. Maybe I can. The Harry Shades Detective Agency, where I work, it's a private firm. You understand? We require payment up front. A retainer. You got to pay us."

"I understand. I ain't addled. Figured I might be needing to grease someone's wheels before anything would happen. Lucky for you, missy, I got heaps of money. Follow me."

I got up and stretched my bad knee. I ambled out the door to the back parking lot in hot pursuit of Dode's worn-denim backside. He moved at a mighty speed for someone so old. His right hip had been busted, so he walked a tad sideways like a crab, but he moved fast.

We stopped alongside the back tailgate of his cherry-red '57 short-bed Ford. He dropped the gate and pointed to a pair of five-gallon glass jars wrapped in moldy newspapers. They looked like something the Jolly Green Giant would use to store moonshine.

I recognized the jars from the sixties, when the Bold Mold Plastics Factory had come to town. Bold Mold used the jars to transport the acid used to clean the plastic auto button molds. In the seventies enterprising folks lugged the jars out of the town dump. Sawed off the tops. Made terrariums. Terrariums were big in the early seventies. People were gaga over earthy things. Ferns in bottles were big. My cousin Betty had a craft barn down in Orleans. She hit the jackpot turning those jars into bottle gardens with teeny plastic gnomes living inside. She sold the whole kit and caboodle to some hippie college students from Vincennes University back in '73. Got enough to retire to a trailer park in Hollywood, Florida. She mails me Christmas cards with palm trees. And she always writes the same darn thing inside: "Eighty degrees here. You enjoying the snow? Ha! Ha!" That Betty always was a smart ass.

Dode pointed at the jars. "Dug 'em up last night in my springhouse cellar. You're working for me now, ain't ya?"

I peeled back moldy newspaper and inspected the jars. The outsides were smeared with clay and dirt. Inside, they were stuffed with coins, or what looked to be coins, mostly quarters and dimes, some pennies, floating around in greenish water.

"Been storing these in my cellar. First National Bank of Dode. Saving them for the crash."

I knew by "the crash," he meant the next Great Depression. He wasn't the only farmer in town who didn't trust banks. Lots of old timers buried the family silver in their cellars or slid silver coin money under the barn floorboards. "How much is in them two jars?" I asked.

He shrugged, wiped the back of his hand under his nose. He took a pinch of chaw from the pocket of his overalls and poked it expertly into one jaw. "Don't rightly know," he said, after sucking the chaw for a moment. "Maybe thousands. Them coins have silver and copper. They don't use real silver no more. Coins today are made up out of allow-u-minimum. Might as well be lead." He spat.

I contemplated the jars. They were full. I contemplated the Shades' Detective Agency bank account. It was empty. We had no other clients. And I'd been holding my paycheck all week because I knew it'd not clear the bank. "Sold," I said as I took hold of a jar and started monkey-walking it to the edge of the tailgate.

Harry Shades, my boss, wasn't going to be happy about this. He'd been perturbed to the point of spitting a couple of months back when Veenie Goens, my best gal pal and fellow sleuth-in-training, had accepted a lifetime pledge of free eggs from Ma Horton in exchange for our sleuthing services. I figured Harry would take the cash, though. He'd said more than once that the Shades agency ought to represent everyone. "Everybody's money is green," was his big motto. Thanks to all the corroded copper pennies, Dode's money couldn't have been any greener. It was dirty money, but I figured Veenie and I could launder it up.

"You're working for me now, ain't ya?" Dode asked again as he helped me roll the second jar onto the tailgate.

"Reckon I am," I said.

"Hot diggity!" screeched Dode. "Just wait 'til them ghosts get a gander at you. Bet they never met a real live ghost hunter. This is just like hiring one of them Hardy boys, except you're a lady, and all."

It wasn't the ghosts I was worried about. It was the boss, but I figured ghost busting was as reputable as most things he got us into. Veenie and I had been outwitting the living citizens of Knobby Waters, Indiana for a while now.

How much smarter could the dead be?

Chapter Two

Yep, Harry was not happy.

Veenie, on the other hand, was bouncing around the office like a balloon someone had let the air out of. Veenie—Lavinia Goens by birth—had always wanted to be a professional ghost buster. Veenie is four feet, seven inches and weighs one hundred fifty pounds. She is seventy-one years old and has white hair she wears swept up kewpie doll style. When she bounces, it makes an impression.

That day she was wearing her customary poncho—this one was hot pink with purple tassels—with fetching yellow capris and a pair of secondhand Wonder Woman Crocs. She'd snatched up the entire ensemble for five dollars in the chubby girls' department at Goodwill.

Veenie and I have been best pals since we worked side by side on the auto button line at the Bold Mold Plastics factory back in the sixties, when we were both still in high school, before the EPA decided that pouring plastic waste into White River was a doo-doo of an idea. These days, jobs are scarce out here in the country, which is pretty much how Veenie and I came to be working for Harry.

Harry was sitting at his desk looking disgusted with the both of us. "No," he said, all sour-faced. "Absolutely not. No ghost busting." He tilted his brown fedora hat back on his head. Unsatisfied that he'd made enough of a statement, he tossed the hat on the desk. He made a sound with his lips like a motorboat.

"Why in tarnation not?" I had to ask.

"Because, for starters, ghosts don't exist." He ran a hand through his pewter-colored hair and straightened his stubby wide tie. He was wearing his customary three-piece suit. He was a trim guy, on the right side of sixty, with a penchant for the married ladies. He'd just grown a moustache and liked to chew on it when he got upset. He was all right mostly but was always trying to class up the business and romance the womenfolk of Pawpaw County. Since no one in Knobby Waters cared much for class, let alone romance, he was pretty much as frustrated as a sick squirrel most of the time.

Veenie had calmed down and was inspecting the money jars. She had a tea towel and was wiping off the moldy newspaper and clay dirt. We'd both officially retired awhile back, but the economy being the way it was, we'd taken a shared job as detectives-in-training with Harry. Pay wasn't much, but it helped. Veenie and I didn't have any 401(k)s or IRAs, or any of those other fancy financial things, but we still had our wits about us. Veenie was a born snoop, delighted at long last to have her natural talents recognized at a professional level. Veenie and I shared a house and a car ('60 Chevy Impala, turquoise). Like me, she was used to living on a budget. The thought of spending the afternoon cleaning the corroded money didn't bother either of us. We were used to working for our money.

"How much you reckon is in them jars?" Veenie asked.

"Dode says thousands."

Harry sighed. "Dode also thinks there are aliens with big butts hanging out in his neighbor's apple trees."

"Or ghosts," I said. "He hired us to determine which. And to make sure they weren't up to no good."

Veenie's little cornflower-blue eyes shone over the top of her Coke bottle glasses. She had some macular degeneration but wasn't about to let that slow her down. Her desire to snoop won out over every infirmity God tossed her way. "I bet it's them Wyatts, come back to haunt the town."

Harry, who was a transplant from up north—South Bend to be exact—asked Veenie why the Wyatts would want to haunt anyone in Knobby Waters.

"They were a bunch of ne'er-do-wells. That's how they got that mansion in the first place."

"What mansion?"

"The Wyatt mansion," said Veenie. "The abandoned one, across from Dode's farm."

Harry snorted. "That thing looks like something the Munsters wouldn't live in. I'd not call that a mansion."

"Well," said Veenie, "it's been empty since the twenties. It's old. Place needs to be gussied up a bit."

I dove into the history of the Wyatt family for Harry. "Jedidiah Wyatt was one of the founding fathers of Knobby Waters. Came up from the South after the Civil War. He operated the first ferry that crossed over from old Fort Vallonia to the Knobby Waters bottomlands. Built the first bank to trade animal pelts and tobacco, stuff like that. From there on he pretty much ruled the roost, back in the late 1800s."

The southern part of Indiana is mounded with hills, shot through with creeks and rivers that bleed south to the Ohio River. You could get on a raft in Knobby Waters, ride it all the way down to Louisville, then hang a right to catch the Ohio River. Once on the Ohio, you could row west toward the mighty Mississippi. Once on the Mississippi, you could shoot straight down to New Orleans. You'd eventually get spit out into the Gulf of Mexico. Most folks these days never left the state, though. It was the river highways that made Knobby Waters a natural trading post with a rich river bottomland suited to tobacco and corn farming back in the day.

Harry looked confused about Jedidiah Wyatt and the geography of southern Indiana. "Jedidiah built the First National Bank of Knobby Waters, Indiana?"

"Heck no," I corrected him. "The First National was the second bank in Knobby Waters. The Apple family founded that one long about 1910. The Apple's bank was the second bank in town, but it made it through all the crashes and bank failures because Silas Apple was so tight he could squeeze a buffalo nickel until the buffalo pooped."

Veenie was nodding along. She looked at Harry. "Didn't they teach you any Indiana history up there in the big city of South Bend?"

"Oh geez," said Harry, "guess I missed the chapter on the founding of Knobby Waters."

Veenie stuck her false teeth out at Harry.

"Oh for Pete's sake, stop it you two," I said. "I ain't got time to babysit."

Harry asked me what happened to the Wyatts and their bank.

"Well," I continued, "the bank and old man Wyatt were long gone before I was born. Bank failed long about 1920. Jedidiah Wyatt claimed the flood of 1919, worst the town ever seen, ruined all the crops and swept away the livestock. All his loans were to farmers. Once the collateral got swept away Jedidiah bolted the bank doors and rowed out of town. When the town folks blew open the safe hoping to get their savings back, the only things in there were an empty whiskey jug, nudie photos, and a note that read, 'Adios, folks.'"

Harry looked dubious. "He just up and left his bank? His house? Weren't they worth something?"

"Turned out the Wyatt mansion, a big old brick Victorian with turrets, thirteen rooms, one of them an indoor bathroom with a blue marble john imported all the way from Italy, was owned full out by some railroad bank and trust down in

Louisville. The bank building had been mortgaged too. All Jedidiah left behind was a mountain of bad debt."

"And his young wife," added Veenie. "Jedidiah was a bachelor until he hit seventy. My pappy told me he'd just married one of those cross-eyed Ollis girls, probably for the dowry. Don't think anyone ever married an Ollis unless they got paid to do it. I know I wouldn't."

Harry petted the end of his moustache. "She related to the Ollises who live out on the brick plant hill road today?"

"Might be," I said.

Harry seemed to be softening up.

"We can take Dode's case? You approve?"

"I wouldn't go so far as to use the word 'approve,' but we are low on cash right now."

"Low?" screeched Veenie. "RJ and I are holding our paychecks. Last week we barely made hot dog money."

Harry stood up and headed toward the door. The detective agency was in an old Rexall drugstore, and Harry lived upstairs in a bachelor apartment, so if he truly wanted to get away from us, he had to scoot out of the office for the day. "Fine. You two take this one. Good training for you. It's lunchtime. I'm headed over to Pokey's to drum up business."

Pokey's was the tavern and pool hall. They served a light lunch. The best things on the menu were their cheesy mystery meat sandwiches and cheap tap beer: Schlitz or Pabst Blue Ribbon. And, oh yeah, their greasy fat onion rings. Men hung out there, mostly playing cards and hiding from their wives. Veenie enjoyed their take-out. Women weren't all that welcome to hang inside unless they were Jezebels, or hard-drinkers, preferably both. On occasion Veenie had called in a late night order of onion rings and a cheesy mystery meat sandwich or two. Pokey's was the only place in town besides the Go Go Gas that was open past midnight.

As soon as Harry was gone, Veenie and I figured out how to pop open one of the money jars. It had been plugged with cork and wax-coated newspaper. The corkscrew on my Swiss Army knife did the trick right nice.

I'd never seen Veenie so excited about a case. She wasn't too happy about the smell that came out of the jars though. "Smells like the cab of Pappy's truck when he used to go fishing in July. He'd toss the catfish in the cab and forget about them for a day or two."

"Worse," I said as I teetered backward, slapped in the face by the smell. I got a jug of vinegar, a bucket, and a little scrub brush from the broom closet, so we could launder the cash.

The top opening on the jug was only about an inch wide. "How we going to get the cash out?" asked Veenie, who, being impulsive, already had her plump fingers stuck in the opening.

"Bust the jar, I reckon."

I dug around in my desk until I found a ball peen hammer. I swung at the jar and it cracked. Water and coins rushed out onto the wood floor. The mess puddled across Veenie's feet like a slimy green tongue.

"Good thing I'm wearing my water-resistant Wonder Woman Crocs," said Veenie.

Wonder Woman squished over to the broom closet to get the dust pan and broom to sweep up the cash.

We sat at our desks sorting the loot in heaps by denomination. That task took most of the afternoon. We came up with about nine hundred dollars from the first jar, which was enough to make the retainer.

I eyed Veenie. "You want to take this to the bank tomorrow?"
"Sure."

I could tell by the gleam in her eyes—they shone like blue fireflies—that she couldn't wait to annoy uptight Avonelle Apple by dumping a load of corroded green coins onto the bank's spotless marble countertops. Avonelle was President of the First National Bank of Knobby Waters, and Veenie's lifelong enemy. They'd been throwing hissy fits with each other for fifty years—a long story that involving a rigged cat judging contest at the Pawpaw County Fair.

The cash cleaned and counted and safely stashed away in double plastic bags from the Hoosier Feedbag, we locked up the office. Veenie and I headed home, feeling mighty proud that we'd landed a new case. Veenie chattered like a chipmunk all the way home in the Impala. We co-owned the '60 Impala, so I had no choice but to let her ride shotgun. Her bad eyesight had caused her to lose her legal license. It was up to me to chauffer us both around.

"I'm running to the Goodwill first thing in the morning," said Veenie. "Need me some new ghost busting attire."

Personally, I couldn't wait to see what she came up with.

Chapter Three

A herd of stray cats streamed across the gravel road in front of Dode Schneider's farmhouse. They had their tails raised high, like furry rudders. They moved like they knew where they were headed. Must have been two dozen of them. A couple of skinny momma cats batted kittens along. The herd made a beeline toward the Wyatt mansion.

The old Wyatt mansion was a Victorian with towers on each end. Gray slate shingles shone like scaly snake skin on the steep roof. The mansion sat on a hill just outside of town on the twisty, roller-coaster road up the knobs. Slapped together of crumbling red brick from the local brick plant, the house was covered in vines that refused to green up regardless of the season. It looked like the kind of place I'd hang out if I were a ghost, or if I were hiding from the law.

We turned down a rutted dirt path. The Chevy humped along until we reached the turn onto Dode's farm. Apparently Dode didn't believe in mowing his yard. The weeds slapped the bottom of the car as we bumped along. I pulled in beside Dode's red, short-bed Ford.

Dode's farmhouse was a simple place. A story and a half, white frame house with a curved porch that hugged the front entrance like a set of welcoming arms. A curtain of tangled blue morning glories half hid the porch, but not the section to the right of the front door, where a line of rocking chairs sat in the shade.

Dode sat in the rocker closet to the door, a rifle laid across his knees. He was dressed in his customary long-sleeved flannel shirt and bib overalls. He raised one hand and waved at us with the rifle. "Them there ghosts are still there." He pointed the rifle toward the apple orchard across the way that ran along the far side of the Wyatt mansion. "I was up all night keeping an eye on them for you."

Veenie bounced out of the car, eager to get started. She'd scared up a ghost busting outfit at the Goodwill. I was wearing blue jeans and a red camp shirt with flowered canvas sneakers. I looked like a normal old lady headed out to shop at the Wal-Mart. Veenie, who was wearing a white pest-control jumpsuit, a red Indiana University football helmet, and a munitions belt, looked more like she was headed for trouble. Veenie's drab-green military belt was loaded with gadgets. Her BB pistol was stuffed into the belt. She jingled when she walked. She had two tubes of BBs stuck in her belt. I wasn't asking about any of this.

Dode leaned his rifle up against the house and gave us both hearty handshakes. "Made us a pitcher of cold well water," he said. "Go ahead. Have you some."

Veenie pulled a Boy Scout's tin cup out of her munition belt. She flipped up the mouth guard on her helmet and knocked back some water. I made like a little old lady and sipped on one of the Ball jars Dode offered me.

Dode asked Veenie if she was the ghost buster.

"Yep. First official case. I watched some tapes on YouTube. Ghosts aren't all that smart. Ought to have this wrapped up in no time."

Dode's eyes widened. "Ghosts are dim-witted? I imagined them to be smart puppies."

"They're just like us. They was us, but then they got stuck trying to leave their bodies. We just have to help them along."

I had to ask. "Where did you learn that?"

"I figured it out. When you die, there's that tunnel."

Dode leaned forward, all ears. "The one with the big light?"

"Yeah, if you're lucky. You gotta head toward that light fast. Some folks get confused and miss the tunnel."

"Confused? About what?" Dode asked.

"Well, they've lost their arms and legs and they are a'flying all over the place. Probably sputter around a good bit, like firecrackers. So they miss the tunnel and then they have to wait for another light to swing by and pick them up. Probably takes a couple of passes before they get comfortably climbed on board."

Dode nodded thoughtfully. "You think these here ghosts are friendly."

"Probably. Probably just confused. They need us to tell them where to go."

I was listening. All this sounded both harebrained and quite reasonable to me, like most of what Veenie concocted in her head. The two of us had been best pals since the sixties when we ran adjacent plastic molding machines at the Bold Mold factory, so pretty much nothing she said or did fazed me.

Veenie pulled out a notebook and a stubby yellow pencil from one of the large side pockets on her pest-control jumpsuit. The notebook had unicorns on it. The stubby pencil was a county fair freebie from Skinny Davis's hardware store, which had gone out of business back in 1963. "I have to ask you some questions before we map the whole dang place for electrical disturbances. You have any reason to believe these ghosts might be demons?"

"Demons?" Dode scooped up some chaw from a tin and tucked it in one cheek. Brown juice trickled down his chin. He wiped it on the back of his hand. His Adam's apple bobbled up and down, taking his tight collar for a ride.

"Have they threatened you? Tried to push you down the stairs?" Veenie, who was in *Dragnet* mode, was taking notes like a pro.

"Oh gosh darn, no. They mind their own business, mostly. Once or twiced they flashed their big asses this way. That scared me. But no, they ain't tried anything mean-spirited."

"That's good, because sometimes ghosts aren't lost. They know where they are. And they know where they are headed. They drag their ghost tails on this side of eternity for a good reason. Anyone ever murdered or tortured over at that mansion?"

"Gosh darn, no. Don't think so. That place has been empty long as I can remember. Our mama never let us go in that place. Said it was bad luck. Said it was evil, what with old Jedidiah stealing the town blind and abandoning his own newborn kin. Mama always said old Wyatt was a devil, and if we ever went in that place, we'd come back out with the devil burning inside us."

What Dode said rang true. Everybody in town was scared of that old house—too scared to even vandalize the place. As far as everyone in town was concerned, the place wasn't just haunted. It was cursed.

Veenie snapped shut her notebook. "Well, don't you worry your head none. Me and RJ, we'll get to the bottom of this. We're not afraid of no ghosts, are we RJ?"

"Heck no." I hoped I sounded convincing. We'd already deposited the retainer. Now that Veenie had mentioned demons I was feeling more cautious. I'd seen *The Exorcist*. No way I wanted my head to spin around. My arthritis was bad enough without some big-butted demon twisting on my neck.

Veenie stood up and straightened her munitions belt. She looked like General Patton headed into battle. "Those apple trees there, those where the ghosts hang?"

"Yep. Right in the middle. They swing back and forth. They clack a bit too."

I wrinkled my nose. "Clack?"

"Yeah, like maybe they have chains they are swinging. Don't ghosts have chains?"

I looked at Veenie.

"Sure. Some of them do. You ever see them ghosts in the daytime? Anyone else ever go into that house?"

"Nope. The ghosts only come out and hang at night. No one goes in or out over there. Saw what looked to be a fancy-pants county assessor take a peak on the outside yesterday. He just shook his head. Got in his car and drove away. Cats love the place. Other than that, it's a ghost house, for sure."

"Ready, Ruby Jane?" Veenie asked as she tightened her belt.

"I reckon," I said. "You being a pro and all, I'll just follow your lead."

"We'll start out in the orchard. We can check around the yard for open graves. People used to bury their kinfolk in the yard, right alongside the family pets. We got to be on the lookout for stuff like that."

I wasn't going to ask what "stuff like that" meant. I figured I'd find out soon enough. Veenie had a tiny folding shovel strapped to her belt. I figured if we found any suspicious holes, I could roll Veenie down into them. She was smaller and rounder than me; nosier too. I could tie a rope around her, yank her back out if need be.

Veenie bounced in front of me and headed across the yard, her red football helmet barely visible over the tall weeds and goldenrod. For an old lady with a heart condition, she rolled at a remarkable pace.

We burst out of the weeds into a mossy area under the apple trees. Veenie had taken a small black electrical box out of a holster on her munitions belt. The box had a dial. It made a crackling sound like a bad electrical wire. It looked like the thing electricians used to check voltage on electrical boxes. "What in tarnation is that?"

"EMF detector." She scanned the meter across tree trunks. The orchard boasted about twenty gnarled apple trees, most of them scaly with lichen. It was still Spring so while the leaves were out the trees hadn't fully budded yet.

"What's that contraption do?"

"Detects electrical impulses. That's how you tell if you have ghosts sneaking around. They leave electrical waves. Like how a snail leaves a trail of slime. It's called ectoplasm. Looks like green slime at nighttime. Didn't you ever watch *Ghostbusters?*"

"That contraption you got looks like an ordinary voltage meter to me."

"Best I could do on a budget. I asked Harry to get us a real EMF meter, but they cost five hundred dollars."

"What'd he say?"

"Stop pestering me."

We spent a couple of hours poking around in the apple trees. Other than the fact the orchard needed a good pruning, everything looked normal. The trees closest to the house had thin, blackened branches that looked like skeleton fingers to me. A few leaves had budded out. They looked like sharp, green fingernails. "Got anything yet," I asked Veenie as we made our way toward the house. I was getting hot and hungry. I'd made us a picnic lunch. It was wadded up in the bottom of my messenger bag. Boiled eggs. Peanut butter and jelly sandwiches. A liter of Big Red on an ice pack for the both of us.

Veenie stopped scanning tree trunks and blew her nose. The ragweed pollen was getting to her. "Got nothing yet, but that don't mean a thing. Ghosts are sneaky like that. Probably cleaning up after themselves."

The horse flies were out now. And they were lunching on my neck. I swatted a couple. "You hungry?"

Veenie plopped down on the moss under a tree. We made quick work of our lunch while plotting our next move. While Veenie had been scanning trees, I'd been kicking around in the weeds. Nothing too suspicious. A few badass gopher holes smack in the middle of the orchard. Prime gopher territory.

Apples fell off the trees and rolled right straight into their little underground kitchens. There was a pile of old tin and boards heaped up close to the house, but I wasn't up to digging around in that. That hot pile of tin looked like it might be home to some copperhead snakes if ever I saw one. It looked to me that the weeds leading up to the house were downtrodden. The weeds lay down into a narrow path about the size of a cow path or a deer trail. The trail seemed to lead up to the back porch door of the mansion.

I pointed out the grass trail to Veenie as we packed up the wax paper and napkins from our lunch. "You reckon that's a ghost trail?"

Veenie shook her head no. "Ghosts don't have no feet. They float." She drew out her BB pistol and poured in some ammo. She rattled the gun for good measure.

"Cats? Deer?" I asked. Deer loved crab apples. There weren't any apples on the trees yet, but the deer weren't fussy. They gnawed the sweet limb tips just the same.

"Could be."

I eyed the back door to the Wyatt mansion. The window was busted out but solidly boarded over. My eyes traveled across the back porch. Vines held the gray, weathered house in a stranglehold. Lots of things could be living in that house. Even more could have died there. No one had nosed around in that house for a hundred years, and personally I could see why. "You game?" I asked Veenie as I swallowed the last of my Big Red pop.

I didn't have to ask again. Veenie was on her feet clopping toward the back door. She had her hand on the grip of her BB pistol. Whatever lived in the Wyatt mansion had better have its wits about it. It was about to go head-to-head with Lavinia Goens. And in the sixty years I'd known Veenie, that contest had invariably had only one outcome.

Veenie busted a couple of boards off the bottom of the door window with the butt end of her flashlight. She kicked at the door while I twisted at the knob. We grunted and sweated and kicked some more. We threw everything we had at that back door until eventually the rotted boards gave way and we fell straight into what looked to be the kitchen.

So much for sneaking up on the ghosts. They'd have to be dead not to hear the two of us coming.

Veenie charged on.

It was dark and musty inside the house. A long white porcelain sink with a faded red pump handle squatted to our right. A couple of rusty iron skillets hung from the pantry rafters. A single beam of light shot down the hallway into the kitchen. Veenie decided to follow the beam. She had the only flashlight, so I decided to follow her.

Cobwebs clung to our faces as we worked our way down the hall toward the beam of light. The light seemed to be streaming from the sitting parlor. That room faced Dode's farmhouse. Dirty streaks of light poured in through the high windows, which were cracked, boarded up tight from the inside. A limestone fireplace on one end was piled high with half-burnt trash and the cotton stuffing out of an old divan. The place smelled like a mouse piss and cat turd salad. Wallpaper wagged in tongues off the walls. Plaster had cracked off the ceiling and splattered in dusty piles across the wood floor. The place was what you might call a "fixer-upper."

I saw dust flakes and spiders drifting down from the tin ceiling as Veenie swung her light around the room. A creaking sound started up. I bumped into Veenie. We froze together like sweaty melting popsicles. I heard a clacking, and my heart leapt into my throat. I relaxed when I realized the clacking was Veenie's false teeth and not some ghost demon with a chain about to brain us for coming to give him the final directions to hell.

The creaking was coming from a rocking chair that was in full swing. We could see the back of the chair and what looked like the clothed arms of a person resting on the arm rests. We could see the top of a dingy ragged bonnet.

I felt a little odd. Like I might wet my pants.

Veenie charged ahead. Spider webs flew everywhere. The BB pistol popped off. A shower of plaster fell on my head and into my eyes, blinding me.

The rocking chair upended. A skeleton clattered onto the floor. She lay there, her bonnet askew, grinning up at us with rotten teeth.

Something flew past me toward the door. It was fast and white and wheezing. It took me a moment for me to realize it wasn't a ghost, but Veenie.

Chapter Four

V eenie beat me back to Dode's porch by a full five seconds. He'd heard the clattering and commotion and was standing on the top step, rifle raised to one eye. He had the rifle pointed at us as we erupted from the weeds behind his truck.

"Oh, hell! It's us. Don't shoot, Dode!" I screamed.

Veenie was dancing around me screeching the same. "Hold your fire, you old coot!"

Dode lowered his rifle. "What in tarnation?"

Veenie's football helmet had fallen off. Her white hair was spiked up on top of her head. Her face was red and soaked in sweat. She looked like a fat albino woodpecker.

I imagined I looked just as bad. My short white hair was probably sticking straight up like a horsehair cleaning brush. My knees were rubbery and knocking together.

Veenie was wheezing like a broken pump organ.

It took us both a minute to recover.

I stared at Veenie.

She looked at me. "That was a skeleton? Right?"

"I, er, think so."

We were both feeling pretty sheepish.

Dode stepped down and took a long look at us. "You seen them ghosts, didn't you? They chasing you?" He raised his rifle and swung it around at the edge of the goldenrods. He fired a couple of blind rounds into the weeds. Stray cats shot out and bounced across the yard like hairballs.

"We saw a skeleton, Dode," I said, my breath almost back in my body.

"A skeleton chased you?" Dode's eyes were as big as headlights.

Veenie puffed up. "It would have, but we hightailed it out before she could get her spirit going. Ghosts sleep in the daytime."

"Hot diggity!" said Dode. "I knew them were ghosts I'd been seeing."

A siren wailed. A Pawpaw County police cruiser, cherry spinning, slid into the yard almost slamming into Dode's truck.

Devon Hattabaugh, the junior officer in training, sprung out of the car. He hunched down behind the open door, his pistol drawn. He wasn't wearing a cop hat. He was wearing his customary beret, aviator sunglasses, and a tie-dyed T-shirt with a pair of denim knee-knocker shorts. His muttonchop sideburns were bushed out like squirrel tails. He was wearing ankle boots and athletic socks. "Hit the ground!" he squeaked. "Law enforcement! Hit the ground!"

Veenie strolled over to Devon. "Put that thing away."

Devon kept yelling, "Got you ladies covered. Hit the ground! Go down!"

Veenie walked up to him and smacked him up the side of his head with the butt of her BB pistol.

"What the bejeebers!" He rubbed the side of his head with the edge of his beret.

Veenie peered into the cruiser. "Where's Boots? We got us a ghost skeleton. We need a seasoned officer of the law to bring it in."

Devon holstered his pistol. "At a conference. Up at the courthouse. A training on emergency flood evacuations. I'm in charge. Responding to all calls coming out of Knobby Waters today."

"Lucky us," said Veenie, who saw Devon as a pimply-faced community college kid, which he was. Knobby Waters was a small town. Everybody knew everybody and their kin. Both Veenie and I had seen Devon waddling around downtown with a loaded diaper a couple of decades ago. We refused to be ordered around by anyone under fifty, or any man who wore a beret, for that matter.

Devon reluctantly holstered his pistol. "Got a call from dispatch. Said there was gunfire. Called for assistance. Backup."

Dode ambled forward. "That would have been me. I called when I heard the commotion from the mansion. Figured the ladies needed assistance. Didn't know how many ghosts we were dealing with. Could have been a herd of them."

Devon eyed Veenie cautiously.

Veenie squared her shoulders. "You know anything at all about ghosts?"

"No. What? Wait a minute. You called me out here because of ghosts?"

Sensing things were about to go from bad to worse, I intervened. "We found a skeleton in the Wyatt mansion."

"Buried?"

Veenie chortled. "Course not. She was sitting up. In a rocking chair."

"How long she been dead?"

"Long enough she's all bone. No skin."

I could tell by the puzzled look on Devon's face that he was trying to figure out if this sort of thing fell under his jurisdiction. The way I saw it, a dead person was a dead person. The law ought to be interested in any body or part thereof found outside of a cemetery. I said as much to Devon.

"Well, okay," grumbled Devon. He radioed dispatch that he'd arrived on the scene at Dode's place and was going into the mansion to investigate the report of a ghost.

"The report of a what? Of a who?" the dispatcher cackled. I could tell by the voice that it was Bitsy Gorbett, and that she was enjoying this call. She was about our age. Probably hated like heck that little Devon got to boss her around.

"You heard me," said Devon. "And I ain't saying it again." His cheeks were red as peppers as he followed me and Veenie and Dode through the weedy path to the house. We could still hear Bitsy cackling over his radio when we climbed in through the busted back door. When we got to the living room, the skeleton was still there grinning up at us.

"Sure looks dead," said Devon as he took out his flashlight and swung it around the body.

"You reckon?" said Veenie.

"From the looks of her, I'd say she's been dead near a hundred years." He shone his flashlight on her black button-up boots. She was wearing several layers of petticoats under her dress, which looked like it might have once been made of some nice pieces of red velvet. Her hair, what little of it was left, curled from under her bonnet like rat tails.

Devon squatted over the skeleton. He ran his light over the hands. "No rings." He flashed light up and down the body. "No jewelry of any kind."

The little walkie-talkie thing mounted on Devon's shoulder squawked. It was the dispatcher, still laughing. "Sheriff Gibson wants to know if this here ghost call involves Ruby Jane Waskom."

I stepped up and spat at the walkie-talkie as Devon pressed the intercom button. "We got us a body here, Boots. Up at the Wyatt mansion."

Some static, then Boots sighed on the other end. "Course you do, Ruby Jane. Whose body is it?'

"Dunno. Looks to be about a hundred years old. A woman."

"All bones, no skin," shouted Veenie.

Devon spoke into the intercom. "What should I do, boss?"

"Your job," said Boots.

"Roger, er, what's the procedure for a skeleton, boss?"

Boots sighed again. "Call April."

I knew he meant April Trueblood, the county coroner.

"Don't matter how old the body is. She can inspect the scene and bag the body. They'll do an autopsy. Try and get an ID. Determine a cause of death. We don't do anything more unless April rules it foul play."

April arrived about an hour later. She was a petite woman who never wore anything but old jeans, a sock cap, and a stained lab coat, even when off duty. Everybody knew her because her dad, Joe, helped lead the Knobby Waters Corn Shuckers to a win in the Pawpaw County basketball tournament a couple of decades ago. Basketball being God's chosen sport, Joe Trueblood was, and always would be, a Knobby Waters legend.

We were all sitting on Dode's porch sipping well water and sucking on a cold salted dish of cucumbers Dode had whipped up for us when April's white van turned into the farmhouse drive. She hopped out of the van, her medical bag in hand. Her salt and pepper hair flipped up over the rim of her black sock cap. It was humid, but she loved wearing that hat. Told me once it helped keep the creepy stuff and smell out of her hair when she worked.

April heaped her bag and gear on the porch steps and looked around. "You gals got a body for me?" She was wearing square, white, plastic sunglasses with bright green lenses. The top corners were studded with rhinestone daisies. I would have looked silly in something so floozified, but those dime store glasses were cute as kittens on April.

Veenie offered to show April over to the mansion and give her the ten-cent tour of the dearly departed.

I don't know who was more excited, April or Veenie. April was chatting about how she'd never done a forensics analysis on just bones before. She'd have to call in the big guns and ghouls from the Skull and Bones Club in the medical forensics department over at Indiana University for assistance.

Veenie was bouncing up and down talking about ghosts. How we might need a séance to get at the real story. "Dead people love to gab," she assured April. "Ghosts will talk your ear off if you give them half a chance. It's lonely as hell being dead. Hard enough to get someone to pay attention to you when you're alive."

I was sitting on the porch with Dode. He was sprawled out in the rocker, his long arms and legs dangling off the rocker like rubber hoses. He was dead to the world. His rifle was on the floor at his feet. His lips were puffing out air, like a steam locomotive leaving the station. The ghosts had done tuckered him out.

I sipped on my jar of cold well water and wondered who was going to conduct Veenie's upcoming séance. I had an uneasy hunch I already knew the answer.

Chapter Five

It didn't take long for April to remove the skeleton. Veenie helped. She was looking ragged around the edges by the time April left. All that excitement had done her in. I could tell she was envying Dode's snooze-fest on the porch. The sun was a red marble sinking behind a curtain of baby corn stalks as we gathered our stuff and crept off the porch on tiptoe, leaving Dode to nap.

"We got any emergency pie at the house?" asked Veenie, her bright little eyes hopeful as we climbed into the Impala.

I shook my head a woeful no.

"I'm weak as a kitten. My bones are jelly. Can we stop and get us some pie?"

I skidded the Chevy to a stop, cut a gravel donut, and spun back up the twisty, winding road to the knobs. I headed toward Ma and Peepaw Horton's place. The sun was fixing to sit, but Ma and Peepaw operated a pie shed that never closed. It was an old tool shed with a pie pantry on one side, a tiny glass refrigerator for cream pies on the other side. If you had ten bucks, you could pick up a pie anytime. There was a metal sap bucket nailed to the door where you could leave your money. Ma had painted a sign that said "Thou shalt not steal." Underneath, after they'd been robbed once, Peepaw had written, "This means you, knucklehead."

Ma and Peepaw also kept the largest backyard hen house in Pawpaw County. Well, calling it a house might be a wee understatement. Peepaw Horton was an energetic fellow, and

29

Ma loved her chickens. Together they'd fashioned replicas of the White House, the Supreme Court, and the Senate building out of scrap lumber. The buildings were connected with two-by-fours and chicken wire catwalks. It wasn't a chicken house so much as it was an entire Chickenlandia. The whole kit and caboodle was fenced with cyclone wire held up by hand-skinned fence posts. Dewey, the big handsome rooster, was the self-appointed president of Chickenlandia. He crowed on and on about nothing at all hours, like most men. The hens ignored him. They ran around pecking for bugs and gossiping out in front of the Senate, where they nested. The hens were in charge of everybody and everything. Veenie was deathly afraid of chickens (long story about a summer job we once had up at Bundy Brothers Packing, scalding and plucking chickens to make canned soup), so she'd never explored the henhouse compound, but I'd taken the grand tour.

Peepaw Horton threw a one-handed howdy as we pulled in next to the pie shed. He was leaning against the shed on a rickety wooden stepladder with screws sticking out both corners of his mouth. It looked like he'd stuck the screws between his lips so he'd have his hands free to work on a roof repair project. Peepaw was skinny. He had a white buzz cut that he'd not changed since Truman was president. His face was the color and texture of a walnut. He wore a dirty gray bowler hat. His eyes shined like nickels. He was so bowed legged he looked like one of those toy cowboys pre-formed to sit in a horse's saddle.

He gripped a screwdriver in one hand. He was tacking the bottom circle of an aluminum pie pan over a hole up where the bead board on the pie shed met with the corrugated roof. "Varmints," he grunted. "Got into the shed last night. Made a mighty mess of a pecan pie."

Veenie shook her head. "They leave the apple alone? We need us some emergency apple pie."

"Ma baked two. Fresh this morning."

Ma Horton stepped out of the pie shed. She wasn't any-body's mother, people had always called her that because she and Peepaw were kindly to stray animals and outcasts. She wiped her hands on her bibbed apron as she came out of the shed. She was wearing a pair of hearing aids. Black antennae, like on an ant's head, sprouted from the top of each hearing aid. Her thin gray hair was plaited in braids that wound like a spool of thread around the top of her head. She wore a flower print dress with a lace collar. The dress was tucked up under her breasts. She wore leather farm boots, their laces undone halfway. The tongues on the boots flapped when she walked. She was a short woman shaped like an apple who'd decided long ago that she preferred the company of chickens to people. And she made the world's best pies.

"Howdy gals," she said. "Just put some pies out to rest in the shed. Help yourself."

That was all the encouragement Veenie needed. She rolled into the shed and came back with a pie in each hand. "Coconut cream for you. Apple for me." I could see where Veenie had already finger-scooped apple slices out of her pie.

Ma asked me what we were doing up her way.

"Dode Schneider. On a case. Ghosts pestering him over at the Wyatt mansion."

"Or aliens. Could be aliens." Veenie was making a lot of noise. I could hear her having at the pie with her fingers. I decided not to look.

Ma leaned into the Chevy window, her elbows on the hot rim. She adjusted one hearing aid. "Dode ain't been quite right in the head since that snowplow hit him."

"At least he has an excuse." I eyed Veenie.

"That why I heard the cops headed toward Dode's?"

"Probably. You know any reason a ghost might haunt that old Wyatt mansion?"

Ma shook her head. "Place was empty before my time. Most folks don't remember old Jedidiah Wyatt. Those that do got no Godly words for him."

"He have kin?"

"Don't think so. He came up the Ohio on one of them paddle wheeled boats. His kin were over in Georgia, or thereabouts. He moseyed up here with the river rats right after we Yanks ass whooped the South. Married one of them Ollis girls. Stole her and her kin blind. Left her high and dry."

Veenie stopped having at her pie. Half of it was gone. "I feel better," she belched. "Not so weak."

Ma peered over at Veenie. "Emergency pie?"

"Saw something ugly. Had to fortify myself."

Ma looked intrigued. "Whad'ya see?"

"A dead person."

"Anyone we know?"

I jumped in. "Just a skeleton. Pretty darn old from the looks of her. She was wearing button-up shoes and a bonnet and sitting in a rocking chair up in the Wyatt mansion. Just sitting there like she'd had her supper and was fixing to sit by the fire for a spell before bedtime."

Veenie sniffled. "Ghosts got her, we reckon. Demons maybe. We reckon she's been haunting the Wyatt mansion trying to get someone's attention. Wanting someone to give her a decent burial."

Peepaw squeezed his head into the Chevy's window. Next to Ma, mashed together like that, they looked like a pair of dried apple bobbleheads. "You gals want some eggs while you're here?"

"We'll take a dozen if you gather them," Veenie said. "My boy, Junior, always has friends coming over, hanging out, mooching. Them boys are eating us out of house and home."

Ma told Peepaw we'd been ghost hunting for Dode up at the Wyatt mansion. "They found a real live dead person."

Peepaw's eyes brightened. "Anyone we know?"

"Nah," snorted Ma, "a bit older than us."

"That's probably good," said Peepaw. A ruckus started up in the White House. Feathers flew out the Senate coop door. Peepaw shuffled off toward Chickenlandia to see what the fuss was all about. He came back shaking his head and handed us a carton of fresh eggs. "Dewey was trying to mount Ms. Betty Grable."

Ma shook her head. "Betty not in the mood?"

"Not in the least. Dewey's sitting up in a sumac tree sulking like a heartbroken Romeo. Left him to lick his wounds."

Ma leaned into my car window. The batteries must have been waning on her hearing aids. She shouted, "Go on down to the library. Bother Queet. She's got the dope on Knobby Waters' pioneer days. If somebody died or disappeared a hundred years ago, she'd be the one to know all about it."

I thanked Ma for the eggs, the advice, and the emergency pies. And we were off.

Chapter Six

It was bedtime by the time Veenie and I arrived home. I knew the time without consulting a watch because Fergie Junior, Veenie's son was awake. He was rummaging through the icebox in the kitchen. Junior slept days and the wandered around the house all night like a hungry possum.

Junior lived in our basement, between the canned beans and the zucchini relish, despite his having earned two college degrees in musicology. When he worked, which wasn't often, he worked nights. He had a part-time gig writing e-music for an Indianapolis Internet company. He called it music, but it sounded to me and Veenie like a rooster scraping his nuts on barbed wire. We preferred the foot-stomping tunes of Dolly Parton.

Junior also had a band, which he'd formed in the seventies in high school, called the Lonely Lip Lizards. Sorry to report that my grown son Eddie is a guitarist in that band. The Lip Lizards played rock and roll every Thursday and Friday night at Pokey's Tavern and Pool Hall. Every other Saturday they played at the Stumble On Inn over in Ewing.

Junior was standing in his tighty-whitey underwear in the kitchen wearing a tattered wife beater T-shirt. He had one pudgy hand wrapped around a jug of milk, a box of corn flakes clutched in the other. There was no mistaking that he was Veenie's offspring. He was shaped like his mother. Butt naked, he resembled a fleshy beach ball. He had a bushy red moustache that drooped off his lip like a caterpillar. He wore round eye glasses, tinted green in homage to John Lennon. He was draped in silver and turquoise necklaces. Like his mother, he could have used a good bra.

It was Thursday, so I figured he was fueling up before putting on his concert clothes and rolling out to a battle of the bands. Veenie tossed him the carton of eggs Ma had given us. What was left of the apple pie she kept to herself. "You get a job yet?" she asked.

"Why you always got to ask me that?" he whined.

"Why you always living in my basement like some kind of rodent?"

"I had a rough childhood. My therapist says you and daddy, your divorce traumatized me."

Veenie snorted. "What traumatized you was your daddy, him being a shiftless idiot and all."

Fergus Goens Senior owed Veenie forty years of child support. His greatest career achievement had been a year spent drilling holes in the backs of TV sets at the Sylvania plant out at the old Freeman Field up in Seymour. Mostly he lived in his pickup truck with a pack of mangy beagles. He specialized in doing odd jobs at odd hours for odd people. In between he'd managed to climb onto Veenie a couple of times. Fergus Senior liked to shout at Veenie that she should be grateful because he had given her the best gift of her life—that would be Fergie Junior —and that she should be paying *him* for that.

To which Veenie always replied, "Well that's debatable."

Veenie shrugged. "I squeezed you out. Kept you alive. A lot of God's critters eat their young, you know."

Junior slurped corn flakes at the kitchen table. He flicked on his iPad as he sucked up breakfast.

"You know," Veenie said, "you'd enjoy life a heap more if you got a steady job and lowered your expectations. Trouble with your generation is you always wanting to be happy. Happy ain't natural. Look at the *Bible*. Those were not happy people.

Those were grateful people. Grateful they didn't get eaten by
locusts. Grateful when a whale belched them up. Why not go
to work and be miserable every now and then like the rest of
us."

"Got a job. I'm a musician. An artist. I have a right to …"
Junior paused. He fiddled with his iPad. "Hey, this you helping
out the local fuzz?"

Curious, I leaned over and stole a glance at the iPad screen.
It showed the home page of the *Hoosier Squealer* website, the
local gossip rag. A line of pink pigs dressed in purple mini-skirts
did a cancan dance along the top of the screen. There was a
selfie of Veenie wearing her red IU football helmet, arm slung
around the skeleton. They looked like besties, or an ad for the
local funeral home.

"Righteous photo, Ma!" cheered Junior.

Veenie peered at the photo, then at me. "Oops! Don't
know how the *Squealer* got hold of that." Veenie grabbed her
apple pie and made a beeline down the hall. She crashed into
her room. I heard the bolt snap before I could scold her for
releasing case information to the public. Our client agreement
was strict about privacy.

I scrolled through the article online to see if Squeal Daddy
knew more about this case than we did. He was an anonymous
blogger, but he had ears and eyes all over town. He was a
regular Deep Throat when it came to gossip. Everyone in
Pawpaw County feared the *Squealer*. Reading him was way
better than watching Jerry Springer. Plus, he could really whip
an ordinary spit of a story into a lurid tale.

Ghosts Hosting Late Night Orgies at Wyatt Mansion

*Just when you thought things were getting humdrum
and dweedle-dumb in Pawpaw County, it appears
disgruntled ghosts have chosen our fair hamlet as their*

new abode. Moreover, they are misbehaving, as ghosts are known to do. Mr. Dode Schneider has reported that he is being visited nightly by specters partying like there is no tomorrow out under the apple trees next door. The trees are part of the old orchard at the abandoned Wyatt mansion.

Being a good citizen, Dode reported the ghosts to the offices of Sheriff Boots Gibson. Sheriff Gibson was reluctant to comment on this story since he has not himself ever seen a ghost. His junior officer, Devon Hattabaugh (related to the Hattabaughs that live over by the Guthrie Mill, not the Hattabaughs that live in the Pansies and Petunias mobile home park) reported that the Pawpaw County police department is exhausted at present policing the living. "By law we don't have to respond to any calls that come from the dead," wrote Devon in an email to the Squealer late today.

Since the sheriff's office would not dirty their hands, Dode, fearing the ghosts were up to no good and might be headed into town to cause a ruckus, hired the Harry Shades Detective Agency. Mrs. Ruby Jane Waskom (RJ to most all of you) and her co-detective Mrs. Lavinia Goens (Veenie to most all of you), went out to investigate the affair on Dode's behalf. And, low and behold what did they find but a skeleton in the Wyatt family closet. And I'm talking literally here, folks.

Pictured below is Mrs. Lavinia Goens taking custody of the skeleton, which is itself being held pending further investigation at the county morgue by Ms. April Trueblood, our beloved coroner.

"It wasn't difficult," said Lavinia. "She didn't put up much of a fuss." Lavinia says this is her first ghost busting case but hopes it will not be her last. She invites anyone who has experience chatting with the dead to call her for

37

assistance with an upcoming séance at the Wyatt mansion. (Her private number is 812-555-5555.)

Ms. Trueblood, the coroner, confirms that the skeleton is female and about as old as Methuselah himself. She has called in the big guns at the university to do an age analysis and a heap of fancy forensics. Ms. Trueblood requests, in the meantime, if anyone is missing an oldster for them to please contact her office.

The story made no mention of orgies. I figured Squeal Daddy put that in the headline just to get people interested enough to click through to the article and the ads. I was relieved Veenie had not gone on public record about ghosts having sex. The ladies auxiliary at the Baptist church would have been all over me about that one.

The comments at the bottom of the story were as good as the story. "If ghosts are living in Pawpaw County scot-free, the law ought to be intervening. The tax rate in this county sucks. I pay almost a thousand a year for my home, and it ain't even a double-wide. If everybody who squatted here like these here ghost hoboes just paid up, then maybe the school could afford some decent uniforms for the marching band."

I clicked "agreed," and powered down the iPad.

Chapter Seven

We couldn't get a spit of work done the next morning at the office. The phone rang and rang and rang like Christmas bells. It seemed the whole county had read Squeal Daddy's blog on the skeleton and the ghosts. And they'd all decided to ring Veenie to offer their advice and insightful assistance.

Harry kept taking the phone off the hook.

Veenie kept slipping it back into the cradle. "This here is good publicity," said Veenie.

"This here is crazy," said Harry. He had his hat in his hands and was pacing up and down the office. He was so frantic he was wearing holes in the wood. "We're a respectable agency. I got my PI license to protect. You're making us look like a bunch of hillbilly crackpots." He stopped pacing and started chewing on the ragged ends of his moustache.

"Harry," I said, trying to break it up between him and Veenie before she laid some whoop-ass on him, "we're barely making expenses. Dode paid us to investigate, and that's what we're doing."

Harry said he'd had enough. He mushed his hat onto his head and stormed out. Said he'd be at Pokey's if anyone needed him. "Anyone *living*," he added. He slammed the door so hard the plate glass windows of the old Rexall drugstore tinkled like wind chimes.

Me and Veenie shrugged. Harry loved to make a scene. He ought to have been born the Queen of Knobby Waters, a princess at the very least.

The phone rang and Veenie answered. She put it on speakerphone so I could get an earful, and so she'd not have to repeat anything vital. I was feeling hopeful. Maybe our dry spell was passing. Maybe we'd get some new clients out of this free publicity. The hood on the Impala had started smoking on the way to work that morning. Black smoke rolled out when I accelerated. It was like gremlins were under the hood frying bacon. I doubted what was wrong with the old Chevy could be fixed with a roll of duct tape and a can of WD-40, though Veenie would try. The emergency fund in the cookie jar was down to five dollars and twenty-three cents. The elastic was going in my underwear, and I was of the age where I'd really begun to appreciate good quality underpants.

If Harry thought we were crackpots, he should have hung around to listen to the ding-a-lings that called all afternoon. Lolly Shepherd called to say that her mother, Vera, had been missing all weekend from Leisure Hills—could that skeleton be her, just how fast did a body decompose, anyway?—but then she called back ten minutes later to say never mind. Her mom wasn't dead. She'd been out all night making senior whoopee with some hot Elk from Oolitic she'd met at a euchre tournament.

Some young guy with a Donald Duck voice called. He wanted to know if the skeleton had been wearing panties. Veenie hung up on him.

A nut from Sparksville with his own church called to say that he'd been told by God that Veenie was now demonically possessed by a dark she-devil. He said he could grant her salvation, but she'd have to sleep with him at least three times.

Veenie asked how old he was and if he could text her a recent photo.

We were both exhausted by lunchtime. Veenie had just taken the phone off the cradle. We were settling in for a late lunch of bologna and Velveeta cheese double-decker sandwiches and Cheetos when we got a walk-in.

Her hair was puffed up beauty-queen big, like it had been rolled overnight in orange juice cans. It was fire engine red. She dangled a lit cigarette in one hand. Her nails were long and polished purple, sharpened to points like pencils. She was wearing denim stretch capris and a tight purple tube top. Her breasts were impressively perky. Bracelets dangled on both wrists. Not expensive ones. These were cheap and pretty, like those sold at the five-and-dime. She was wearing false eyelashes and enough eyeliner to impress Cleopatra.

"Howdy gals. Name is Kandy Huggins. From the Homer Huggins clan down around Scottsburg. Had a dream told me you gals needed some help up here."

She plopped down in an office chair and lit her cigarette with a monogrammed "K" lighter that she pulled from her purse, a tiny silver thing that dangled on a strap from her shoulder.

Veenie eyed her suspiciously. "What kind of help?"

"Ghosts, specters, that sort of thing." Kandy looked around the office. "Hey, this place is kind of cute. Never been in this neck of the woods before. Had an uncle did time over at Terre Haute, but we never drove through this way. Might have eventually come through this way, but he wasn't there long before they fried him. Some terrible misunderstanding between him and a feeble-minded fella about who owned a squirrel rifle."

I was intrigued. "What do you know about ghosts?"

"I reckon about everything. They talk to me. Right regular too. They give me messages to pass on to their kin and loved ones. Yak! Yak! Yak! I guess you'd say I'm like a switchboard to the Holy Hereafter." She barked out a laugh in a cloud of smoke.

Veenie handed her Harry's special Grand Poohbah Elks water glass to use as an ashtray. "What message you have for us?"

Kandy flicked her cigarette. "The lady ghost, the one attached to that there skeleton you found, says she is mighty grateful you found her. Says she couldn't rest until she had a decent Christian burial. She's been waiting for a hundred years, you know."

Veenie was all ears now.

I was kind of intrigued too. "What else did the skeleton tell you?"

"Said she wants to talk direct, heart-to-heart, to the woman who found her."

Veenie's eyes brightened. "That would be me."

"Well, all righty then. You can set up a séance? Out at that mansion where you found the skeleton?"

"Heck, sure can."

"Here's my cell number." Kandy flipped her cell phone around to show the display to Veenie. The two exchanged cell phone numbers. "Sooner is better. Now that the ghost is kicking around and about to be buried, we don't have a lot of time before she passes over to the other side. Once she's gone, there won't be any forwarding address. I'm staying out at the Moon Glo Motor Lodge, down by the river."

Veenie said, "They still got them vibrating Magic Finger beds?"

"They got lumpy beds." Kandy cradled her lower back. "And the water out there tastes like it's been plumbed from the devil's own hairy ass."

Back in the sixties, the Moon Glo had installed quarter-driven massage beds as a promotional gimmick. People used to meet up there for quickies before going fishing. I reckon they still did. I'd never used one of the Magic Finger beds, but Veenie had once because, well, because she was Veenie and had to try every little weird thing. Her report at the time had been, "It wasn't all that magical. More like a poke and jab. Then the thing tosses you right out of bed."

"Sounds like how your ex, Fergus, used to go at it."

"Yep. Just as magical, but he never charged me a quarter."

Kandy stood up and tried again to straighten out her back. I wondered how old Kandy was. Her clothes said thirty, but her neck crepe screamed fifty. She was kind of flashy, like maybe how you'd expect a carnie fortune-teller to be. I decided to poke at her some more. "You charge money to do a séance?"

"Course I do, honey. I'm a professional. I got expenses." She opened her tiny silver purse and slid a card onto the desk that featured a crystal ball and a picture of her in a blonde wig taken at least twenty years ago. She was wearing gypsy earrings and gazing at the glowing ball. The card said she was a traveling psychic and a fortune-teller.

Veenie jumped in. "How much you charge?"

Kandy looked around the place. I got the sense she was trying to figure out how much she could squeeze out of us before we would squeal. "Two hundred dollars. That's my senior discount. You two are getting on. Closer to the afterlife. Don't require as much energy to dial-up the dead. Don't mind giving you old gals a break."

Veenie considered this. We still had a couple of hundred left on Dode's retainer and his second jar of moldy money as a backup. "We got to ask Dode. It was him who hired us. This would be on his tab."

"Who's that?"

"Dode Schneider. He owns the farm next to the Wyatt mansion. It was him who saw the ghosts and hired us."

Kandy seemed to tuck that little Post-it Note of information into a folder in her mind. I wondered if she saw everything and had talked to the skeleton direct, why didn't she know all about Dode?

I asked, "The ghost of that skeleton tell you her name? How she came to die with her bonnet and dress boots on?"

Kandy popped out her hips and cracked her back until she could stand upright and normal. "Yep. Sure did. I can give you a free sample, but you got to buy a ticket for the rest. Like I said, I got expenses. Just driving over here cost me a ten-spot. And the Moon Glo ain't cheap."

"Lay the sample on us."

She jangled the bracelets on one wrist. "She was murdered. Popped off in her prime. Her name starts with an 'A.' Alta or Allegra or Anabelle. Something old and fussy like that. She's kicking up a fuss in the apple trees because she can't go on over to the other side until she has a Christian burial."

"I knew it!" squealed Veenie.

"Gals, she's asking for your help to save her immortal soul. And to help bring her killer to justice." Kandy's eyes steamed up like maybe she was going to squeeze out some tears, but then Harry came charging in the door, hat in hand.

Harry stopped dead in his tracks when he saw Kandy prancing around. He extended his hand. "Harry Shades, at your service ma'am. This is my agency. These gals treating you right while I was out on a case?" He smoothed back his pewter-colored hair with one hand. He flashed his teeth, which were real and just a tad bit crooked.

Harry had been on a case all right. A case of Schlitz from the smell of him.

Veenie explained why Kandy had visited. "We're going to ask Dode to spring for a séance, help solve the case. Kandy here says it's a murder. I reckon having a séance will get us some good free publicity."

Kandy sidled up to Harry like she'd known him—or his type—all his life. "I'll be in town a couple of days. Staying down by the river at the Moon Glo. Don't see no ring on that manly hand. Maybe we could meet up later? Go over the case?" She batted her eyelashes.

Harry put his hands on his hips. "I know the Moon Glo. Could stop by after work. Could give you my full attention then. Maybe take you out for a spot of dinner at Pokey's downtown."

"Perfect. I just love being escorted. After dinner, I would be needing your *full* attention, of course. Everything you got, sugar."

Harry walked Kandy to the door, looking very pleased with himself.

As soon as she was gone, Veenie pranced around Harry's desk doing a little snake dance with her hips. "Oh Harry," she said, rolling her eyes. "You know where the Moon Glo is, don't you, sugar?"

I chuckled.

"Get back to work!" Harry grunted. He went into the bathroom and slammed shut the door.

Veenie eyed the door. "You think Harry knows he's about to be taken for a ride by a first-class hoochie-coochie gal?"

"Imagine he's dreaming about it right now."

Veenie and I got busy dialing up Dode. He immediately gave his permission to set up a séance that Saturday night.

Chapter Eight

The next morning, we decided to visit Queet Hudsucker, the town librarian, to see what she knew about the Wyatts. The library was on the way to the White River Boat and Gun Club, where Dickie Freeman, Veenie's boy toy, had promised he'd take a peek under the hood of the Impala. The car roared to life just fine but was sending up smoke signals by the time we pulled into the library lot.

Normally Veenie and I lugged around a Chilton manual. We fixed car problems ourselves. But the smell of the smoke and the burning engine was off-putting enough that we figured it might be best to throw a man under the hood. Dickie had been our mechanic over at the Lube It Up. We'd known him since high school. He'd recently retired. He'd do anything for Veenie. Sad to say I wasn't too proud to pimp out my best friend for free auto repair. Not that Veenie minded. She'd always been a little sweet on Dickie.

The old Chevy belched gratefully when we pulled into the gravel lot next to the library and came to a firm stop. The library was in an old yellow brick- and limestone-trim building. It sat on a little rise on a nice green plot of grass, shaded by maple and walnut trees. Someone had hung a children's swing in one of the trees. A steep limestone front entrance staircase was guarded by a pair of lions that looked just like the ones that guarded the New York City Library. Petunia and begonia beds surrounded the building. It was a great place, not changed much from when the Carnegies had first commissioned it. The front double doors were all glass, heavy to hoist open, the doorknobs and railings all polished brass. The only change made in my lifetime was a wheelchair accessibility ramp that had been built off a side entrance. Inside it always smelled like Murphy's Oil Soap and lilacs, and books, of course.

Queet waved as we strolled into the library. She was down on her knees at the end of a row of books, shelving incoming and straightening the rows as she went. She was a touch humpbacked and liked to wear sweaters tied over her shoulders to hide the fact. Her gray shoulder-length hair still had a lot of curl and sass. Today, she was dressed in a red cardigan with white sequin butterflies. Her denim skirt was wide and dragged the ground when she stood up. Scoffed tips of hiking boots peeked out from under the frazzled edge of her skirt. "Hey gals," she called. "Just got some new mysteries. Got that Aussie priest detective you like, Veenie. Father Mackie John."

Veenie scurried over and latched hold of the book. "That Father Mackie John is a little hottie," she said. "I wish he'd toss the cloth and ravish that Irish housekeeper of his, Miss Elizabeth."

A teenage girl, a volunteer library aid, slumped by with a tower of children's picture books. She had white earbuds plugged into both ears. She eyed Veenie suspiciously.

Veenie paid her no mind. She took her Father Mackie mystery book to the checkout counter.

Queet asked what we'd been up to. "Saw that story on the *Hoosier Squealer* site. My, oh my. You gals certainly lead exciting lives. April got anything on that body yet?"

Veenie sniffled as Queet scanned the book. "Nah. We was hoping you might know something. About Jedidiah Wyatt and his kin."

"Got some stuff about them in the Knobby Waters history archives. Most of it isn't scanned. Still in folders. Got a box or two in the town history archives. Let me fetch that stuff for you." Queet scurried away.

Veenie and I sat down in some soft velvety red chairs in the reading room. I started peeling pages on a lady's magazine while Veenie flipped through her new novel looking for the trashy parts. "Oh boy," she said, "listen to this: 'Father Mackie John felt his manhood stiffen when Miss Elizabeth came into his private chambers. Her bosom was swollen with despair ... or was it desire?'"

A young mother dressed in a black-and-gold Purdue T-shirt and white pedal pushers crept over. She put her finger to her lips and made a "shhh!" sound. She pointed to a wall sign that read "This reading room is for the enjoyment of all. Please be quiet and courteous."

Veenie stuck her false teeth out at the woman.

"Well, I never ..."

Veenie said, "Well maybe you ought to. You might feel better if you did."

The woman stormed across the room. She sat down at a table alongside what appeared to be her son, a kid maybe nine years old. He was reading a book about pirates. The woman gave Veenie dagger eyes for a couple of minutes but gave up when Veenie wiggled her ears at her. The woman eventually buried her nose in the current issue of *Good Housekeeping*.

Queet motioned for us to join her in the community room, back by the restrooms and coffee machine. "Got a few things for you gals," she said.

Veenie took the folder from Queet and spilled the contents out onto the table. There were some photos, a couple of tin types, and some regular prints. The documents were mostly legal papers related to the bank and the mansion. "So Jedidiah was real, eh?"

Queet adjusted her reading glasses, which hung on a pearl chain around her neck. "He was very real. Took twenty thousand dollars in gold and silver with him the night he rowed out of town. The bank's last audit and balance sheet is in there, stamped by the regulators up at Indianapolis. That's him. Right there."

Queet pointed to a tintype. Jedidiah Wyatt was sitting stiff as a board in a high-backed velvet padded chair with carved lion's heads on the arms. His face was tiny and wrinkled like a raisin. He had a handlebar moustache waxed to a curl on each end. He was wearing a top hat and a gentleman's silk scarf and brocade vest. He wasn't very tall because the photographer had put a velvet-tufted stool under his feet so they didn't dangle in midair. His boots and spats looked spit-polished. He held a gold-tipped cane like a king's staff in one hand.

Veenie studied the photo. "Snappy dresser," she said. "Must have taken all morning just to dress that moustache. I can't even get Fergie Junior to pull on pants before he goes out on the porch to get the mail."

Queet clucked her tongue. "Yeah. Men used to dress a whole lot better. Now it's all butt crack and hippie whiskers everywhere you go."

I asked about the other photos.

Queet fanned them out. "Here's his wife, Alta Iona Ollis. This is their wedding picture. Married 1919, the week before the flood. He took off in the rowboat that same week. Never even gave her a proper honeymoon. They'd been planning to take a carriage ride down to Louisville, and then on to see the sites in Atlanta. They planned to visit his kinfolk and the Southern lady fashion saloons along the way."

Jedidiah was standing in this photo, one arm draped over the back of the ornately carved chair where his wife sat. She was trussed up in ten miles of lace. Her cheeks were puffy, like those of a child. Her long light hair had been curled with an iron so the ringlets fell down onto her exposed bosom. Her right eye was a little lazy.

Veenie commented. "Holy corn dog. Kandy, that's a medium we done hired, said the ghost was named something with an 'A.' She even mentioned the name Alta. Why, she was just a baby. Walleyed as a pike to boot. What happened to her?"

"Nothing good, sorry to say," said Queet. "There's a paper in there attesting that she lost her mind when Jedidiah left her. She was ordered consigned to the Indiana Hospital for the Insane in Corydon. Melancholy, the reports says."

"That's rough," I said. "How long she in there?"

"Probably died there. Place closed down after a fire in the seventies. Most of the records were lost. Back then people lived in asylums until they died. What cures they had—opium, cocaine, laudanum, lobotomies—were far worse than the diseases. You thinking your skeleton might be her?"

I mused. "Could be, but if she was committed and locked up down in Corydon, how'd she get back here? And what killed her? She have any local kin who might remember her story? Aren't the Ollises out on the brick plant road a part of her clan?"

"Think so. Got a genealogy chart. Brought in by a fellow named Randy Ollis. I think he'd be Alta Iona's brother, Jeb's, great-great-nephew. Alta had but one brother, Jeb Ollis. Big lumber tycoon. Stripped the farmland down in the Knobby Waters bottoms. Ordered corn seed from South America. Went on to plant corn. Lost it all in the bank failure and Alta's dowry to Jedidiah."

Veenie studied the yellowed papers. "Well, lookie here. This here chart says Alta Iona had a daughter, Myrtle Mae Wyatt, born eight months after Jedidiah skedaddled. Reckon the old coot gave her a bit of a honeymoon after all."

We all stared at the birth certificate. Jedidiah was listed as the father. "Anything else you can tell us?" I asked Queet.

"It's all pretty much in that folder. Randy Ollis brought that folder in back when we started the history archive. Said we ought to have this stuff. No one in his family was interested in keeping it. Said the mice were chewing it up. Glad he thought to bring it in. What happened back then was an important part of Pawpaw County history. Banks weren't regulated then. That didn't happen until after the big stock market crash, under FDR."

Someone rapped on the conference room door. It was a man wearing Birkenstocks, a straw hat, and a rucksack. He said he had some books to donate for the library sale later in the month. Queet excused herself. Told us to leave the file folder on the table and she'd reshelf it later.

I asked Veenie, "Should we pay Randy Ollis a visit?"

"Yep. Think so." Veenie checked her cell phone. There was a text from Dickie Freeman. He wanted to know if we could meet him out at the Boat and Gun Club early. He had a proctology appointment later in the afternoon and wanted to make sure there was time for him to crawl under the hood of the Impala and give it a once over before the proctologist did the same to him.

Veenie texted him back, "Sure thing, honey buns," and we were on our way.

Chapter Nine

The White River Boat and Gun Club is not hoity-toity, unless you were born in Pawpaw County. If so, the place is pretty much a yacht club and the country club all rolled up into one. Its events were the height of the Knobby Waters social scene, especially in the summer months when fishing and hunting were in full swing.

The clubhouse is your basic fishing camp bunkhouse, made of tacked-together, gray weathered wood with a mossy tin roof. Inside, under exposed rafters, a handful of chipped folding tables were strewn about. There was a kitchen in the back with white metal cabinets where fish fries were held in the summer and bake sales for 4-H and the Boy Scouts were held in the fall. A wide screened porch wrapped around the clubhouse. Fly strips loaded with winged bugs twisted like big yellow corkscrews in the river breeze that blew around the porch. Rocking chairs and hammocks were scattered haphazardly along the porch. The clubhouse sat on stilts on the sandy lip of the White River. It was nested in an elbow bend in the East Fork of the White River, where Greasy Creek trickled into the main waterway. Sycamores, weeping willows, box elders, and a sprinkling of maples shaded the wide chocolate-colored water. Clouds of mosquitos hung over the place. Not far in the distance you could see the covered bridge and the tractor turn off road to the Moon Glo Motor Lodge.

When we arrived, Sheriff Boots Gibson was sitting on a dented, red pop cooler, fishing off the end of the porch. He had on a cowboy hat and his customary blue jeans. He cast a long line and then shot us a one-handed wave. The deep, wide channel he was casting into was known as the Greasy Creek catfish honey hole. Legends had been caught off that porch. According to the fishermen and women of Pawpaw County, some of the catfish that flipped and dove in that deep hole were big enough to saddle up and ride.

We waved back at Boots.

Veenie said, "Your boy Grape Nuts Gibson don't look all that happy to see us."

Veenie had been calling Boots Gibson "Grape Nuts" since we were kids hanging together in Vacation Bible School. Boots got hold of some grape Kool-Aid powder out of the rectory kitchen, licked his fingers, and ate off the sugary purple mess, then later latched onto himself to take a leak. The rest was local legend. He wasn't that fond of the nickname himself. Preferred Boots.

"He'll get over it. We're making him work for a living. You know how he hates that."

"You ought to date the poor fellow, put him out of his gosh-darn misery."

Boots had been in love with me since second grade, or so said the rumor mill. I'd been married once. My husband, Charlie "Whiskers" Waskom, had died suddenly. His ticker burst on him twenty years ago, right in the middle of his drawing up a farm insurance quote. He'd gone face down in a bowl of German potato salad during the closing pitch. He traveled express lane to the Holy Hereafter, just like that. I'd grieved over him for a good couple years. Then one day I woke up and suddenly felt pretty, well, OK. Marriage, in hindsight, had been a heap of work. I didn't plan on having any more amorous entanglements. I had two all right kids, all grown. I pretty much liked being a lone wolf at this state of the game. If I ever had to revisit the sex stage of my life, I was planning on making it a DIY project.

"I don't want to date. I'm leaving that to you and Sassy," I said to Veenie. "I get all the lurid excitement I need just watching the two of you." "Sassy" Sue Ann Smith was a divorcee our age who rented a room from us. She'd recently returned to town from California and was working her way through anything that could still stand and take a leak. We hadn't seen her at the house lately, so she must have trapped someone who thought she was worth feeding and watering for a few days. She was that kind of woman—an ace at husband hunting.

Dickie Freeman hopped up the steps and greeted us. We'd both known him for a coon's age. He was widowed and a few years younger than Veenie. He was cute as a button and easy going. Trim little guy. Loved to dance. Still had some strawberry-blond hair nested above his ears. Dimples the size of Clark Gable. He called Veenie his little firecracker and loved poking at her until she sputtered. He carried a dented, green metal toolbox in one hand. "Want me to give the old Impala a once over, gals?"

We nodded and followed him down the steps to the back sand lot where the Chevy was parked under some willows. A swarm of black river flies floated after us. When we got to the car, Veenie reached under the front seat and yanked out a spray can of WD-40. She let go at the flies. They fell to the ground like wet, oily raisins. She got the WD-40 on my glasses, and I ended up groping around in the glove compartment looking for some napkins to wipe off the oil. I found a lace garter (not mine, and I wasn't about to ask Veenie) and managed to smear my glasses clean enough to see Dickie.

Dickie popped the hood and stuck half his body under there while I ignited the Impala.

Smoke rolled out like one of those Chinese black snake coils we used to light on the sidewalk during Fourth of July as kids.

Dickie stumbled backward and waved the smell from his face. "Lord, God, Jesus in heaven, what have you gals been doing? It smells like you've been boiling possum on this engine block."

Veenie stuck her head out the window of the Chevy. "Is that bad?"

Dickie made a face. "When was the last time you had an inspection?"

I leaned forward and squinted at the sticker on the windshield. "Two years ago?"

"Oh heck. You're driving illegally, you realize."

Veenie jumped in. "We're not illegal. She has a driver's license."

Dickie shook his head and wiped his hands on a red shop rag. "Car has to be inspected every year, gals. You know that."

I did know that, but since Dickie had retired, I didn't like my odds of the Impala passing an inspection. Spike Hill, the young guy who bought the Lube It Up from Dickie, had two fishing hooks in his bottom lip and abnormally short arms and legs. He looked like something that belonged in a circus. And he did not appear the least bit susceptible to my senior charms. "Can't you inspect it for us?"

"Could. Maybe. The boys still like me down at the Lube It Up. But you're going to need a whole new radiator. Some engine work. She's burning a butt load of oil."

Veenie looked at me accusatively. "This is because you buy that cheap gas at the Korean Go Go. That place is run by Ruskies. You know the Koreans are plotting to blow us up again. You ought to buy Phillips 66 Flight Fuel. That stuff runs rockets."

"Phillips 66 don't exist no more," I said. "Also, stop picking at me, Lavinia. Dickie said he could fix it."

"No problem," said Dickie, checking his watch. "But can't do it today. Got to order a radiator. Talk to Spike about reserving a bay to do the work. It could take a week." He slammed shut the hood.

Veenie smooched him up. "Thanks, honey bun."

"You bet, sweet pea," he said in return.

I rolled my eyes.

I went to back out of the sand lot, but Boots Gibson was standing square behind me, hands on hips. One hand was holding a string of catfish, his catch for the day.

"Uh, oh," Veenie said. "Busted!"

Boots strolled up and peered in my window.

"You want to see my license?" I said.

"Smart ass," he said.

Veenie piped up. "We weren't doing anything illegal."

Boots moved his head farther through the window. "Lavinia, the way you say that makes me think you were."

"Oh for Pete's sake, what is it you want Boots?"

"Well, I was going to tell you that April called. She has a cause of death on that skeleton. But I reckon I won't be pestering you two anymore."

"Boots!" I called. "You come straight back here."

He did.

"Tell us what April said."

"Well, all the tests aren't back yet, but she has some things down pat. First off, the skeleton was a young woman."

"We figured as much from the clothes."

Veenie piped up. "Could have been one of them crossdressers. J. Edgar Hoover wore ball gowns. Pumps too. If he'd died in one of them getups, you might have thought he was Queen Victoria or some other horse-faced old lady."

Ignoring Veenie, Boots continued. "Died of arsenic poisoning. Big hits of the stuff in her hair and nails. Just thought you'd like to know this is now an official county murder investigation."

"About time," Veenie said. "We told you something bad was going down out there at that mansion."

"Horse patootie," said Boots. "That woman died a century ago. If she was killed—and that is a hell of a big if—whoever did it is long gone. You just created a mess of paperwork for me. Plus, I got to listen to Devon chatter on and on about how he's a cold case forensics expert now. He's strutting around in his beret like he's the star of *CSI: Knobby Waters*. I may have to take him out to my back forty and shoot him just to gain some peace and quiet."

Veenie leaned forward. "You got any suspects?"

"Heck no. We don't even know who the woman is yet. They're plugging her DNA into the convicted felon's database. They're hoping to get some match that will tell us her local kin line."

"I bet it's Alta Iona."

"Alta Iona?" asked Boots.

"Alta Iona Ollis," I said. "She was Jedidiah's young wife. He took her dowry with him along with the contents of the bank vault when he rowed out of town in 1919."

Veenie piped up. "She went batshit crazy when he betrayed her. Stole her family fortune and her heart. Left her knocked up. Sent her to the insane asylum. Locked her up like a loony."

Boots made a face. "Then how'd she get back here?"

"We don't know," I said.

Veenie said, "We're holding a séance to ask her."

"A séance?"

"Yep. We got us a professional medium. We're setting her up out at the Wyatt mansion so we can talk directly to Alta. Solve the mystery."

"No, you're not," said Boots. "You're definitely not doing that."

Veenie leaned over. "You're not the boss of me, Grape Nuts Gibson."

The Sheriff clutched his badge. "This here says I am, Lavinia."

Oh boy. If Veenie didn't shut up, I was going to be visiting her in the county jail and taking her sharp spoons and shit so she could tunnel out. I asked Boots why we couldn't have a séance.

"That mansion is a crime scene now. No one can enter that property unless they are working for the state forensics team. Thanks to you two, it's going to take months to get through all the red tape on this case."

That shut Veenie up.

Me too, for a spell.

"I'll be off now," said Boots. He took his string of fish and sauntered over to his pickup truck. He tossed the fish into the cooler in the back bed and eased out of the sand lot onto the gravel road back to town.

"Well," I said.

"Well," echoed Veenie.

"I think we've been put in our place."

"We certainly have been."

"Totally."

I fired up the Impala. Smoke steamed off the hood.

"Where we going Ruby Jane?" Veenie asked.

"To see Randy Ollis."

Veenie's little eyes brightened.

"I'm thinking maybe he knows something about Alta. Then I think we need to call up Dode and Kandy. Arrange what time the séance ought to be. Arrange to pick up Kandy tomorrow night so we can get this dog and pony show on the road."

Veenie flashed a grin. "Bootsie boy won't like that."

"Probably not. Definitely not. But it doesn't really matter what Bootsie boy likes. We're not inviting him to this little shindig," I said as I swung the Chevy up the steep brick plant hill road.

Chapter Ten

Randy Ollis's house was on the left behind the brick plant, just past the blue gill pond. It wasn't really a house. More like two trailers snuggled close to each other on cement blocks. The trailers were from the sixties. One was two-toned aqua and white. The other had been painted with black spots and had horns mounted on the front. I think it was meant to be a cow. A pair of plaid sofas nested in the tall weeds in the front yard, and several abandoned cars circled the sofas. A row of shanty-style dog houses lined the dirt driveway. Black-and-tan hounds ran back and forth on a chain run. They yelped at us as we got out of the car. The black and tans were coon dogs. Coon hunting was a big sport in this part of the country.

Veenie stopped to pet the dogs. That just made them holler more.

A man stepped through the screen door on the cow trailer. He had long, tangled brown hair, like Jesus, and he was wearing a hooded Indiana Pacers sweatshirt. His knees poked out of his worn blue jeans. He stood in his bare feet on a stack of cement blocks that served as the stairs into the trailer, squinting, trying to decide if he knew us. His hands were tucked under his armpits like maybe he was cold.

"Howdy!" Veenie said.

The man squinted some more. "You ladies lost?"

"Nope," I said. "Not if you're Randy Ollis."

"The one and only." He grinned. He had a nice smile. "Hush it up!" he yelled at the dogs, which had started baying again. "Pardon them," he said. "They don't get much company. What can I do for you ladies?"

He looked us over good, like he was checking to see if we were carrying bibles or *Watch Tower* magazines.

"We're here about Alta Ollis."

"Lord, she's dead. Long time now." He scratched the side of his nose.

Veenie stepped forward. "We think we found her. Out at the Wyatt mansion."

"No shit? Hey, wait. That skeleton? I knew you looked familiar. You're that old lady ghost hunter from the *Squealer*, ain't ya?"

Veenie puffed up. "Yep. That's me."

"You think that skeleton is my kinfolk. Aunt Alta Iona?"

"We do," I said. "We tracked you down from that file folder of stuff you left at the library."

"Holy shit," he said. He put his hand to his eyes to shade them and peered out up and down the road. "Is this going to be on one of them unsolved crime TV shows? Shit, I just love those shows."

"Might be," said Veenie. "Can we come in? Ask you some more about Alta?"

"Er," he danced on his bare feet. "I reckon. I live alone. Divorced. Just me and the dogs. Place is a mess. Don't get much company out this way."

Veenie and I hopped up the cement-block steps and into the trailer. It was dark inside and smelled wet. The stale air was heavy with cigarette smoke and mold. The plywood walls were plastered in posters of Dale Earnhardt Junior and Danica Patrick. A paint-by-numbers oil painting that featured two dogs hunting hung askew above the sofa. The wall on the right of that, toward the kitchen, featured a glass rifle case with one of the two doors missing. The case held three rifles and several stacked boxes of ammo.

Randy ran a hand along the sofa, knocking off a pile of clothes, hunting magazines, and some Papa John's pizza boxes. He brushed crumbs off the puffy sofa and offered us a seat. "You ladies want something to drink?" he asked as he cracked his knuckles. "I got water. And beer. PBR."

I said I was fine, but Veenie took a cold PBR. He slipped it into a foam koozie with a NASCAR logo on it, so it'd stay cold and not slip out of her little hand.

A window air conditioner was running. It was loud and sounded a lot like a cat trying to cough up a metal hairball. Randy had placed a rusted roasting pan under the window to catch a line of drip from the air conditioner.

"Nice place you got," said Veenie.

"Oh thanks. Not much, but it's home. Wife got the house in the divorce. I rent out the other trailer. Brings in a little income. I work the second shift at the foundry over in Bedford."

Veenie sipped her beer. "You ever hear tell what happened between Alta and Jedidiah Wyatt?"

"Oh sure. Family still talks about it. We was rich folk once. A family don't forget something like that." His Adam's apple bobbed as he took a swallow of beer.

I asked if Alta had died in the asylum down in Corydon.

"Nope. In fact, she never made it there. You know about the baby, right?"

"Tell us," I said.

"Well, old Jedidiah knocked up Aunt Alta, if you'll excuse my French. Then he left her high and dry. Not much else to tell."

"The papers you left at the library included a commitment order sentencing Alta to the state asylum in Corydon. Your great-great-granddad, her brother, had Alta Iona committed?"

"Oh he tried, sure enough." Randy took a pull on his beer and swept the hair back from his eyes. "But she holed up in that half-done house. Refused to go. No one knew she was pregnant but her. When the baby came, she went batshit crazy. They took that baby. Sent it to the orphanage up in Brownstown. My family would have kept it, but it was a girl." He took a pull on his beer. "And they were busted broke. Robbed blind by Jedidiah. No money to feed another mouth. Back then, nobody wanted a girl."

"You know what happened to that baby girl?"

"Nope." He took a big swallow on his beer. "I think she got adopted by some well-to-do folks over in Brownstown who couldn't have a baby, but I don't know names. Never seen records. I think everybody decided out of sight, out of mind. Back then people didn't tell kids they was adopted. She probably didn't even know."

"Your family still own the old Wyatt mansion?"

"Heck no." Some bank down in Louisville, or maybe Jeffersonville, anyway some big bank held the mortgage. They got the thing lock, stock, and barrel. Guess they couldn't sell it, or else they went under too in the Depression. I think the county owns the place now. Back taxes. Not right sure."

I was curious about the arsenic poisoning Boots had told us about. "Anyone ever tell you that Jedidiah killed Alta?"

"Oh heck, no. Why you ask?"

"April Trueblood, the coroner, says that skeleton was loaded with arsenic."

He whistled. "Man this is just exactly like one of those unsolved TV mysteries. I wish I knew what happened to her. I was told she wouldn't go to the asylum. They took that baby girl to the orphanage, her begging them not to. You think that rascal killed her, huh?"

"Hard to tell, but we'll let you know what we find out." I stood up. "Don't want to take up more of your time. Appreciate your yacking with us."

"Not a problem." Randy kicked us a path to the door. He held open the screen door. "I will tell you, some folks, my grandpa Ollis mostly, used to go on and on about how there was a treasure buried out there at that old place."

Veenie popped up under Randy's arm at the door. "A treasure?"

"Yeah," he chuckled. "Can you imagine that? It's the same way folks say those Reno brothers who robbed that train up around Seymour must have buried the gold somewhere. People been digging for the Reno brothers' lost gold since the Civil War ended."

Every Hoosier schoolkid knew the Reno Brothers legend. The world's first train robbery had been in Seymour, Indiana in 1866, just after the Civil War. Simeon Reno and his brother John and their friend John Sparks boarded a train and made off with a safe full of gold. They robbed three trains. Most of the loot, well over one hundred thousand dollars in gold, was never recovered. People still walk those train tracks out to Hangman's Crossing and down the fields, swinging their metal detectors as they go.

Veenie said, "Well who wouldn't want a safe full of gold?"

"What makes people think Jedidiah buried anything?" I said.

Randy danced on his cold bare feet on the cement-block step. He shoved his hands down into the front pockets of his jeans. "Legend has it there should have been twenty thousand in that safe between townsfolk making trade deposits and Alta's cash dowry. But that safe was empty. Bank auditors never recovered one itty-bitty penny."

"You think there's any truth in that story?"

"I reckon there's some truth in every story." He smiled. "Don't make much difference now. That all happened long ago. I imagine if Jedidiah was like most of us, he took everything he could grab in that rowboat when he hightailed it out of town."

"Where'd Jedidiah go?" Veenie asked.

The coon dogs started baying again as we crossed the yard. Veenie stopped to pet them.

Randy followed us out to the Impala in his bare feet. He tossed the dogs some biscuits from a can nailed high to a fence post. "Nobody knows where Jedidiah went. Some say back down south to Georgia or Alabama where his people came from. Some say Mexico. Same say he died in the flood. He just disappeared. Never to be seen or heard from again."

"Like a ghost," said Veenie.

"I reckon," laughed Randy. He tapped on the top of the car and stepped back as I ignited the engine.

Smoke curled out from under the hood.

Randy pinched his nose shut and hopped back from the car. "You ladies might want to have that looked at," he shouted. "Smells like trouble."

The dogs howled again.

Veenie gave Randy the double thumbs up as we zoomed away.

Chapter Eleven

I woke up with Veenie sitting on my bed, poking at me. "You awake? Ruby Jane. You awake?"

I rolled over and eyed her. "Dang it, Veenie, I am now."

"We got to go over to Pokey's."

I rubbed my eyes. They were fuzzy with sleep. I clicked on the bedside lamp. "What time is it?"

"Nighttime."

"What's this about? You hungry?" I sat up and shucked off my sleeping pants. I pulled on a pair of jeans and an Indiana State sweatshirt from the rocker by my bed. I always dumped my clothes on the rocker on the way to bed. Most women my age folded their clothes neatly at bedtime. I'd given up on all that neat stuff during menopause. During menopause everything fell apart on me. I figured it was no use trying to project orderliness, what with my body and the whole universe conspiring against me. I decided to join hands with the chaos. I'd been much happier since.

"Junior called. Needs a ride home from Pokey's. Someone stole his Harley."

"Oh for Pete's sake. He sure it was stolen? Last time he called like this, he'd just forgotten where he'd parked it. He sound stoned?" I let my hands fumble over the nightstand searching for my eyeglasses.

"He sounded like he always sounded, whiney. I told him to call up one of them Goobers."

"You mean Ubers?"

"Yeah, but he says they won't come out to Pokey's no more. They got robbed too many times. Says his new friend needs a place to crash too. Could we take him in?"

"Lordie, where we going to hang another living soul? The hallway closet?" I slid my feet into my sneakers. They were flowered canvas slip-ons. I was past the age when I wanted to bend down and tie my shoes every day.

"Maybe he's a little person. He might fit in the dryer." Veenie seemed awake and eager to chat. "We got any emergency money in the cookie jar?" She sat on the edge of the bed and swung her little feet back and forth, scaring up some dust bunnies.

"Some," I said. I wasn't going to ask why she asked that question because I already knew.

I trotted to the kitchen, Veenie in tow. I fished into the cookie jar as we went out by the back kitchen door. I pulled out a twenty and a couple of crumpled ones. Not much, but more than we'd had in there for a couple of months. Dode's ghost problem had plumped up our Twinkie fund.

Veenie plucked the bills out of my hand. "Could use me a cheesy mystery meat sub. Some fat onion rings. Make the trip downtown worth the effort." She smoothed the bills and tucked them neatly into her bra.

Pokey's Tavern and Pool Hall is in an old brick building built in 1896. It was the only business in Knobby Waters, other than the First National Bank, that had never gone bankrupt or been closed. My daddy used to say if you had to invest in something, invest in good liquor, because no matter how bad times got, men would always find the money for a cold one. People bought liquor in good times to celebrate their lives and in bad times to commiserate. Five generations of Knobby Waters patrons had worn the wooden barstools to a shine inside Pokey's.

When we strutted into Pokey's, it was after one in the morning. The crowd was thin. Not like it was ever that thick, mind you, except for March Madness during the basketball playoffs. That time of year men tumbled like dung beetles over each other trying to get into the bar. Fistfights broke out over a prime barstool to sit and watch the action on the big screen that hung on rusty old tractor tire chains from the rafters.

The air inside Pokey's was thick with smoke and the smell of fried onions. The glow of neon from the tavern sign and the beer ads lit up the place in red-and-green streaks. The juke box was on, and Kenny Rogers was wailing. The sound of pool balls cracking together ricocheted through the smoke.

Harry, the boss, and Kandy the medium, were holed up in a corner booth making out. Harry's hat was on the table. A row of dirty highball glasses lined the lip of the booth. A mess of dirty dishes, a half-eaten red plastic basket of onion rings, and a greasy trail of used paper napkins spilled across the tabletop.

Veenie made a disgusting sucking sound as we walked up to Harry's booth.

Kandy popped up for air. "Howdy, gals." She looked like a heartbroken raccoon. Her eyeliner was running. She finger-fluffed her red hair, which was mashed down on one side from working her way up Harry's skinny neck like a human Hoover.

Harry waved a bottle of Schlitz at us. His tie was loose. His jacket and vest were off, and his shirt was unbuttoned down to his sternum. He was one of those guys who had a freckled, smooth chest.

Veenie eyed Kandy. "We got the séance all set up with Dode for tomorrow night. Me and RJ will pick you up at the Moon Glo, long about seven."

Kandy pulled a cigarette out from a silver case in her tiny purse. "You gals got cash money?"

"Sure."

"Can I see it?" She held her hand out, palm up. She rubbed her fingers together.

"Nope," said Veenie.

"Why not?"

"It's in the bank. Harry will write you a check once we get the ghost talking. This here is a business transaction. We pay on satisfactory completion of service."

Harry raised his beer. "I'm good for it, baby."

Fergie Junior was fooling around up on the music stage. He was breaking down the microphone and speakers. A guy next to Junior was sliding his guitar into a battered case that was plastered with seventies band stickers.

"Yo! Ma!" Junior waved. "Thanks for the ride."

"What in the name of Sam Hill happened to your hog?" asked Veenie.

Junior shrugged. "I parked in the alley next to the dumpster. It's gone now." He shuffled around disconnecting the mics.

"You sure about that? 'Cause last time you called us for a ride that Harley was parked over at the bank, right where you left it."

"I'm sure. Don't I look sober to you?" He stepped up and whipped off his green John Lennon glasses. His blue eyes were a little bloodshot, but the pupils were normal, not fly specks or full dark moons. Even his reddish moustache looked straight and sober, neatly trimmed on the ends for a change.

The man who'd been packing up his guitar behind Junior stepped forward and offered his hand to Veenie. I'd seen him sneaking in and out of Junior's basement hidey-hole twice during the last week. "Pleased to meet you, ma'am. I'm Darnell. Darnell Zikes, from down around Washington County."

Darnell was short and pudgy with one lazy brown eye. He wore plaid white and blue pedal pushers and a wife beater T-shirt that read, "Save a horse. Ride a redneck." His feet were stuffed into Dr. Scholl's slide sandals. White athletic tube socks puddled around his thick ankles. His face looked like someone had mashed gravel into his cheeks. His gray hair, held back by a yellow paisley bandana, was stringy and tangled like a well-used mop head. Tiny Willy Nelson style pigtails framed the side of his face.

Veenie eyed Darnell. "Aren't you a little old for rock-and-roll?"

Darnell puckered up. He toked on a lit doobie he snagged from a nearby ashtray. His eyes squinted against the smoke. "I dunno, let me consult with Mick Jagger. Get back to you on that, Granny." He coughed out a laugh.

"He's the same age as me, Ma," said Junior as he slipped into a sleeveless jean jacket. A puff of reddish gray hair, like a mouse, stuck up in the V of his "High Powered," black T-shirt.

"Like I said," grumbled Veenie.

Junior shuffled his feet. "It ok if Darnell crashes with us a few days? He's passing though. Filling in for Eddie."

"What the heck is wrong with Eddie?" I was tempted to add *now*, because my grown son always moped around. He was pushing fifty. Like Junior, he'd somehow got the notion in his head that life was supposed to be a heap of fun. He wrote poetry and cried an awful lot for a grown guy. I'd never known what to do for him, God bless his little achy-breaky heart.

"Er, nothing wrong, not really," said Junior. "I mean, he's just feeling poorly. His gal dumped him."

"Didn't know he had a gal," I said.

"Well, he don't now."

Veenie was sitting on a stool at the bar chatting up the owner of Pokey's Tavern, Pokey Tatlock. She was putting in her take-out order for a mystery meat sub and some fat, hot, greasy onion rings.

Pokey had huge blue anchors tattooed on each bicep, like Popeye. Busty mermaids swung on the anchors. He was as tall and broad shouldered as a football player. He was the type of guy who loved many, but married none. At least thirteen kids in Pawpaw County had his chin dimple, but not a single woman ever wore his wedding ring. His hair was jet black and he kept it greased back like a sixties heart throb. A spit curl fell over his forehead in a Clark Gable, devilish sort of way. He was growing white at the temples, but that didn't seem to affect his popularity with the women.

I went over to see what Veenie was up to while I waited for Junior and Darnell to pack up the band. They got free food, a sort of all-you-can-stomach buffet deal, in exchange for playing at Pokey's. They were snorting up the leftovers on the hot bar. Darnell was busy spearing onion rings on his pudgy fingers, shoveling them down his pie hole. Between bites, Darnell was squirting ketchup into his mouth. Junior took to imitating him. I hoped to God they didn't upchuck in the Impala on the way home.

"Ruby Jane," said Pokey. He grabbed my hand in a hearty two-handed shake. "Looking good, gal."

"You too, Pokey. What's the news?"

"Got nothing on you two. Saw that piece in the *Squealer*. Ghost busting, man, you gals really know how to party."

"It's Veenie," I said. "Trouble follows her around like a piglet waddling after its mama."

Veenie grinned. "It's my special talent."

"Say," said Pokey. "I got me a mystery. Maybe you two gals could help me solve it."

"Lay it on us."

"Someone's been breaking into my back pantry. Eating my profits. I can show you, if you got a minute." He hitched his thumb toward the back pantry. "Dinner's on me, if you'll have a look."

Pokey popped up the hinged part of the bar, and we scooted under and followed him past the potato chip racks and candy bar displays toward the kitchen. We went through the kitchen where his mom, Dolly, was shaking the onion ring fryers and using a spatula to beat on some mystery meat. She was a tiny woman, older than us. She was wearing a Marilyn Monroe blonde wig and smoking a Virginia Slims cigarette. She was wearing cat-eye glasses that were greased over with fryer spittle. Her earrings dangled like fishing lures from her earlobes. She had to stand on a step stool to reach the grill. Dolly tossed us a wave, but kept right on working the grill and fryer with both hands as we slid by.

"Your mama's looking mighty good," I said to Pokey.

"I keep telling her she don't need to work no more. Me and the boys can support her, but she loves work. Always thinking up new surprise dishes. Last week she made an apple, Snickers bar and baby marshmallows salad with an Oreo crumble crust. Boy, that stuff flew out of the refrigerator."

"Sorry I missed that," said Veenie. "Sounds healthy. Got all your basic food groups. Nothing healthier than apples and nuts. And chocolate, that's a health food now too."

We were standing in the pantry. The back door opened out into the alley. A little side window was cracked open, letting in air. Outside the window the alley was lined with gray dumpsters. Several businesses, including the Hoosier Feedbag Grocery and the sheriff's office, shared those dumpsters with the tavern.

The pantry was narrow and tall. One side was lined with shelves covered in tacked-down oilcloth. Pokey stored trays of buns, big white buckets of potatoes, and institutional-sized bags of sugar and flour on the shelves. A see-in, sliding door refrigerator held tomatoes, lettuce, slaw, mayonnaise, giant yellow cheese food loafs, and a couple of gallons of iced tea with lemon wedges floating in them like little yellow canoes. A white lowboy freezer held, I was guessing, meat patties and bags of onion rings and other fried food delicacies. Several dented, untapped kegs of beer were rolled tight to the wall.

Veenie eyed it all. "What's the problem?"

"This here is the problem," said Pokey. He shoved aside some giant plastic bottles of ketchup.

We stared at a bag of hot dog buns that had been ripped open. Bun pieces were tossed everywhere. A super-sized bag of BBQ chips had been ripped wide open. The shelf was dusted in red BBQ powder.

Pokey shook his head. "Mama cleaned up most of the mess. It's like this every morning. Some mornings worse. Been going on all week. Plus," he walked over to the lowboy freezer and popped open the lid. Cold steam rolled out. "We're missing several bags of mystery meat."

Veenie had to stand on tiptoe to see in the freezer. Her glasses frosted over. She took them off and wiped them on her shirttail. "Varmints?"

"Nah," said Pokey as he slammed shut the freezer lid. "Varmints couldn't open the freezer and take out the meat."

I looked around the freezer, then behind it. "They take the bags whole? No sign they are dragging them out and eating them here?"

Pokey shook his head.

Veenie pointed to some tiny footprints in the BBQ powder on the shelf and some nibbled holes in the buns' plastic bags. "Looks mousy to me."

"Sure," confirmed Pokey. "I mean, we got mice. Who don't? But that don't explain the missing meat. It'd take an army of mice to spring that freezer and shoulder out those bags. Those bags are clean gone. Where'd they go?"

I eyed the little window at the far end of the pantry. It was open an inch or so. Too small for a grown person to climb through. "You leave that window open at night?"

"Sure, during the day we blow it wide open. Open the door into the kitchen too so Mama can get a breeze going. Don't want her fainting, going face down into a fryer."

I eyed the distance between the window and door. "It's a small window. Wouldn't stop the dumpster raccoons, though. They could reach right in. Twist open the doorknob."

Veenie nodded. "She's right. Raccoons have them creepy little hands. They can open refrigerators. Open jars. We had a pack once that got in at the VFW. Opened all the jars of peanut butter. Came in one morning, found a pair of them sitting on the kitchen table with five-gallon peanut butter jars stuck on their heads."

Pokey crossed his arms, and his tattooed mermaids wiggled. "How do you explain this? Can a raccoon do this?"

He walked over to the metal keg nearest the door. There was a puddle of yellow beer on the floor.

I saw instantly what he meant. The keg had been tapped. Someone had taken off the cardboard protective cover and screwed down a tap system and pumped up some beer. The floor was puddled with overflow.

Veenie inspected the tap. "Somebody sure knew what he was doing."

"Yeah," said Pokey. "It's a neat tap."

"Also, Veenie eyed the other kegs, "they got taste. They tapped the PBR. That's the good stuff."

Pokey wiped his hands on his apron. He shut the door to the pantry as he led us out. "You gals think you can solve this here mystery?"

"Sure," said Veenie as Dolly handed us a white paper bag with the top neatly rolled down. It contained our to-go order. The onion rings were already staining the bag with giant spots of grease. "Let us think on it for a spell."

"You got it," said Pokey. "And hey," he said, as he swatted Veenie on the ass, "don't be strangers. I owe you gals, and Big Pokey always pays his bills."

Chapter Twelve

Junior's new friend, Darnell Zikes, crooned all the way home. Something about bow-legged women and broken cowboy hearts. The boys were crowded in the back of the Impala with their drums and guitar cases. When I squinted in the rearview, Darnell looked like some homely girl Junior had picked up. I reckoned it was the Willy Nelson pigtails.

Darnell leaned up and rested his chin on the front seat between Veenie and me. He put me in the mind of a gray, floppy-eared dog. He started pestering Veenie about our ghost busting case. "You seen ghosts?" he asked. "For real? Real dang ghosts? I mean, how do you know they was ghosts, and not like moonbeams or clouds or some such shit?"

Darnell seemed like a nice enough fellow, but his stray brown eye made it hard to concentrate on what he was saying. I kept an eye on him in the rearview as we chugged home. Fergie Junior wasn't the best judge of character. He had a good heart, but left unsupervised, he often showed a real affinity for redneck riffraff. He once brought home a sweet old hobo he met at a Grateful Dead concert at the State Fair up in Indianapolis. Turned out the guy was wanted on three charges of cannibalism down in Kentucky. I wasn't happy about the wacky weed he and Darnell were toking in the back seat, but at least it kept them mellow.

Veenie chattered on about our ghost case between bites of her cheesy mystery meat sandwich. "We found the skeleton. That's as good as a ghost. We reckon the ghost belongs to the skeleton." She wiped her chin with a paper napkin. "Want an onion ring, RJ?" she asked.

"Sure." Though I knew I'd regret it as soon as I lay down in bed later.

Veenie squirted two packages of ketchup on a giant ring. She held it out to the side of my mouth like she was offering it to a dog. She knew I wasn't about to take my hands off the wheel. I gnawed off the crunchy burnt crust. I sucked in the slippery onion as I cautiously rolled through the four-way stop in the center of town.

Veenie continued explaining the case to Darnell. "Coroner says the skeleton was murdered. Poison. Arsenic."

"No shit?" said Darnell. "For real?" He exhaled a cloud of smoke that rivaled what had been coming from under the hood of the Chevy lately. He handed the doobie to Junior. "Who was she? Who murdered her?"

"Don't know. We're thinking she was Jedidiah Wyatt's wife, Alta Iona. Maybe old Jedidiah offed her."

"I thought he up and left town. That's what that Internet guy wrote."

"Nobody knows. That's why we're having a séance. We need to talk to Alta Iona ourselves."

"You find anything else out at that mansion?"

"Like?"

"I dunno. Like anything cool. Flying saucers? Mummies? Cool stuff?"

"Nah," said Veenie. "But we didn't really get to poke around. Once the coroner came, the fuzz roped it off as a crime scene."

Too late, I saw the sheriff's car hiding behind a dump truck in the parking lot at the Guthrie Mill. He'd been hiding waiting for speeders or late-night drunks. The red light whirled on. A siren chirped. The cop car pulled out after us.

Darnell panicked. "What the fuck! Hey, the cops are after us. Hit the gas, Granny!"

Veenie sucked down the last of her mystery meat sandwich and licked her fingers. "You're paranoid," she said. "It's the wacky weed. Hang loose. And keep your yapper zipped."

I pulled the Impala onto the gravel shoulder and glanced in the back seat. "For Pete's sake, try and look innocent," I said to the boys. Junior nodded and sat up straight. Too straight. He looked like a corpse wearing John Lennon glasses. He folded his hands in his lap. He tried to whistle, but his lips were too dry. They fluttered like paper.

Darnell's one stray eye looked guilty. No matter how hard he tried, that eye bounced around the back seat like a brown Super Ball on speed.

Great. All Veenie and I needed was to get busted for possession.

I watched as Boots unfolded out of the sheriff's car. He moseyed up to the Impala. He pulled his long leather ticket book out of his back pocket. "Evening, gals," he said. "What you doing out so late?"

I reluctantly cranked down my window.

Veenie leaned over me and waved at Boots. "Hi, Bootsie. Snack run. Down at Pokey's."

Boots eyed me. "You gals been drinking?"

"Course not."

He leaned in closer and sniffed the car. "Smoking?"

"For Pete's sake, Boots," I crowed. "I'm pushing seventy. The only drugs we do come with a prescription."

Boots twisted his head until he could see in the back seat. "That you, Junior?"

Junior murmured, "Hello," and waved shyly.

"Who's your new gal pal?" Boots asked Junior.

Darnell squeaked up. "I'm a guy."

"Oh sorry. It's the pigtails."

"Willie Nelson wears them."

"Yeah, and a sight better than you, son," said Boots. "What's your name, boy?"

Darnell puffed up. "Nunya."

"Nunya what?" asked Boots. He had his flashlight out of his belt and was shining it around the back seat.

"Nunya damn business."

That was definitely not the right thing to say to Boots. "Step out of the car, son."

Boots was at the back door of the Chevy, opening it now.

Darnell slid out of the car.

Boots ran his light beam up and down Darnell's body. He looked a little messy and stoned standing there in his pigtails, plaid pedal pushers, and sloppy socks.

"You from out of town?" Boots asked.

"Just across the river. Washington County."

"Why you here?"

"Passing through. Stopped to wet my whistle. Got some dinner over at Pokey's. Junior needed a guitar man. Helping him out in exchange for a crash pad."

Boots shined the light on Junior's eyes. "That true?"

Junior kept his tinted glasses on and nodded yes.

Veenie piped up. "He's staying at our place. We can vouch for him while he's in town."

Boots grunted. "That supposed to make me feel better?" He asked Darnell for a driver's license. Darnell fumbled around until he got a brown leather biker's wallet pried out of his back pocket. It was attached to his belt loop with a chain. He sprung it open. A bunch of Post-it Notes and condoms spilled out onto the ground.

Boots eyed the condoms, ran his flashlight beam over them, but said nothing.

Veenie peered up over my shoulder. She stared out at the condoms. One of them had a black wrapper with a picture of Batman on it.

"You got any Wolverine willie warmers?" Veenie asked Darnell. "I like that Wolverine. Boy, that wolf man could ravish me anytime. How-l-l-l!"

Fergie Junior groaned from the backseat. "Ma!"

Darnell nervously petted the ends of his pigtails.

Boots handed Darnell back his license. "How'd you get to town?"

"Bus. Like I said, just passing through. Got cousins up in Gnaw Bone. Hope to get a job with them. Own a junkyard up that way. I do auto body work when I'm not strumming."

I was getting sleepy. And grumpy. "Why'd you pull us over, Boots?"

"You ran that stop." He nodded back to the four-way in the middle of town.

"Rolling stop," I corrected. "And tarnation, Boots, there isn't another living soul awake this time of night."

"I am."

Veenie peered over at Boots and said, "You want an onion ring?" She dangled two on her little finger.

"That from Pokey's?"

"Sure is."

Boots took the onion ring and crunched on it. "Okay. Guess you gals can go. But next time I'm writing you a ticket. We got laws. You can't be hot-rodding around town breaking the law just because you're old."

Darnell crawled back into the car. "What the fuck was that, man?" He craned his head around and watched Boots until the siren on the squad car whooped off and the car slid back into the shadows behind a dump truck in the lot at Guthrie's Mill.

"Old people flirting," said Veenie as she tossed back a fistful of Tums. "Bootsie has a crush on Ruby Jane, but she won't put out. Won't even talk to him unless he whips out his gun and badge. Poor guy has a bad case of country-fried blue balls."

"Veenie," I said, as we pulled into our driveway. I was already beginning to regret eating those onion rings. A belch the size of a basketball was rumbling up my esophagus. Something big was fixing to happen on the other end too.

"What?"

"Shut your pie hole or else you'll be riding your bike to work all next week."

Chapter Thirteen

It was late afternoon Saturday when Veenie and I spun onto the dirt road that led along the river to the Moon Glo Motor Lodge. We were headed to pick up Kandy for the séance. The motor lodge sign was up, but it no longer lit up at night. The neon that used to advertise "Magic Finger beds" had fizzled out long ago, probably about the same time as disco and my sex drive.

A pair of turkey buzzards had built a big old straw and mud nest on top of the word "Magic" in the neon sign. The mother bird appeared to be sitting on some eggs. She craned her ugly, red, bald head around as we bumped along past the sign. I had a feeling she was hoping we might be dinner.

"Lookie there," said Veenie. "This place is a real love nest."

"They could mow the road," I bellyached as I squinted into the sun.

"Them high weeds are deliberate," said Veenie. "Darn smart marketing."

"How's that?" I flipped down the visor and squinted some more.

"The tall weeds keep it discrete. Private. Romantic."

"Romantic might be one word for it. Personally, anything mating in weeds this high I hope never to see naked."

I pulled the Chevy tight to the office door. The motor lodge was painted bright white with grass-green trim. The paint blistered from the concrete building in giant boils. A metal "Vacancy" sign squeaked back and forth in the river breeze. A sign under the "Vacancy" sign read "Air Conditioned," though someone had scrawled "NOT" in front of that. A hand-lettered cardboard sign tacked to the door read "$20 nite. $10 hour." The front door was thrown open, and the inner screen door was propped open with a rusty spade with a cracked handle that looked to be permanently driven into the ground. At one time there might have been a flower bed in front of the office, but now there was just a scattering of cigarette butts trying to take seed.

The motor lodge consisted of ten rooms jutted out in a line from the right side of the office, with a narrow porch shading the entrance to the rooms. Metal scallop-backed chairs painted grass green sat along the walk, one by the side of each door. A double-bay ice machine chained shut with a combination padlock featured a sign that read "night crawlers $2." I reckoned they meant worms for fishing, but based on the looks of the place, all sorts of things might be crawling around the Moon Glo Motor Lodge after dark, none of which I'd pay two dollars to meet up with.

"What room is Kandy holed up in?" I asked Veenie.

"Didn't say."

I climbed out of the Chevy and ambled up to the office. A man with a Buddha belly was sitting on an orange plastic sofa in the lobby. He was wearing camouflage cargo shorts and no shirt and was sunburned. His chest was covered in shaggy gray hair, and he wore plastic flip-flops and square, purple, plastic glasses way too big for his face. He held a sweating diet Coke can in one hand and a TV remote in the other and was squinting up at a small TV that sat on a shelf in the corner. A cigarette smoldered in a glass ashtray on a Formica table in front of him. The Formica had orange and black melted burn marks along the edges where people had left cigarettes to burn over the years. *Gunsmoke* was on the TV screen.

"Excuse me," I said. "Sir."

He took a hit off his cigarette, his eyes glued to the TV. "Yeah?"

"I'm looking for someone."

"Ain't we all, sugar?" He exhaled but kept his eyes on the TV. "Leave your cash on the counter. No need to register. It's the twenty-first century. No one gives a shit anymore."

"It's a woman. I'm looking for a woman," I said.

"Like I said, be as weird as you like, sugar, no one cares. Room two is empty. Linens are clean. Key's on the wall behind the counter. Help yourself."

Veenie popped into the office behind me. "It's hot as the devil's hairy ass out here." She sniffed the stale office air. "And it smells like foot fungus in here. What's the hold up?"

Veenie was dressed in a new Goodwill outfit. She'd settled on a mystic seventies theme for the séance. Lime green, wide-legged culottes with a pair of purple Converse ankle sneakers and a white, leather, beaded vest with a shaggy lime turtleneck. The back of the vest had what looked to be gravy stains, but Veenie figured she could rub those out with a little white shoe polish. She'd been wrong. She looked like some kind of seventies yeti.

The office clerk looked up. "Cripes! You old gals swingers? Look, if there's gonna be more than two of you, that's five dollars extra. You'll use more towels. Old people use a lot of towels. You horny seniors use too much lube."

Veenie yanked the cord to the TV out of the wall.

"Ah, man, why'd you do that?"

"We're looking for a woman. Kandy Huggins."

"Oh yeah. She registered under an alias, Kandy Cane. Must be her. Room one. Not very creative, but then, we then we don't get a lot of high IQ guests out this way. You ladies hookers? Not like I care, but I got an old pal up at Leisure Hills who's having a ninetieth birthday party this week. We could use some cheap entertainment."

"We're not hookers," said Veenie. "We're hip."

"If you say so." He plugged the TV back in and went back to watching his programs.

Veenie and I strolled down to room one. Veenie pounded on the door. When she got no answer, she lugged a metal chair over and tossed it against the door.

The door creaked open. A white oval face peered out. It was the boss, Harry. He was wearing a woman's kimono robe with a loud flower pattern and elbow-length sleeves. The robe showcased his skinny legs and knock-knees. His pewter-colored hair had sprouted a rooster tail in the back. His moustache was drooping in the humidity.

"Where'd you get that classy robe?" asked Veenie.

Harry blinked. "Kandy." He tossed one shoulder backward. "She's got taste."

"Not in men, she don't," Veenie said.

Kandy appeared in the doorway. She was fully dressed, fiddling with fastening a silver-loop earring big enough to be a horse's nose ring. She was wearing a long, ruffled, red skirt and an off-the-shoulder peasant blouse. "Hi gals. Almost ready. I finished a good while back, but Harry there is like a little Energizer Bunny. Keeps going and going and going." She barked out a laugh in a cloud of smoke. "Boy, put a quarter in his bed stand and you sure get your money's worth."

Harry smirked like he was proud of himself.

Veenie slid in under Harry's arm, not waiting to be invited in. Harry's robe fell open revealing a yellow thong and a thin line of gray hair, like marching ants, which trailed from his belly button down into his thong.

"Put your pants on, Harry. No one wants to see that."

He grabbed his pants and suit jacket and hobbled to the bathroom.

The room was tiny, barely big enough for two people to stand between the bed and the TV. The TV was an older, fatter model cradled in a metal roller stand. The mismatched bed sheets were twisted like a tornado had flung them around the room. The TV was on, but the sound was off. The room smelled like wet towels, bleached underpants, and some sort of cheap floral air freshener.

Veenie sniffed the place. "Not as romantic as I remember."

Kandy shrugged. "Seen worse. Seen better. The bathroom is real clean. No mold in the shower. Plenty of toilet paper. They even have fancy two-ply nose tissues."

Veenie made herself at home on the bed. She jumped up and down, testing the mattress. Dust flew. Thick clouds full of mites, hair, dry skin, cooties, and God knows what else. Her vest fringe flew like little white doves through the clouds of dust. "I couldn't make whoopee on a mattress like this. Nope. Too many pokey springs. I got me one of them newfangled pillow top foam mattresses. It's like doing it on top of a bowl of marshmallows."

"Yeah," said Kandy. "Those are real good."

Veenie clasped her hands together in her lap. "You feeling psychic?"

Kandy was standing at a full-length mirror slathering on pink lipstick. She puckered. Blotted. Slathered some more. "Think so. Always helps when I have good sex. Gets my juices flowing." Kandy tossed her hair and shoulders and did a little hoochie dance. Her silver and gold dangle bracelets clattered like gypsy clackers.

Harry strode out of the bathroom. His hair was slicked back, his tie tied, his jacket slung over one arm. He was carrying his fedora hat in his free hand. He looked as happy as a puppy with two peckers. He gave Kandy a little pat on her behind. "Ready to do some voodoo, sugar buns?"

Kandy grabbed her little silver shoulder purse and we all ambled out the door like a herd of turtles. Kandy was a little unsteady on her high heels, and Harry walked like he'd been ridden hard and put away wet. The sky was turning black as we settled into the Impala. Fist-sized clouds were rolling up the river. Thunder rumbled in the distance. The willow trees along the river had begun whooshing in the wind like squirrel tails.

"Oh boy!" cried Veenie. "I feel itchy. I can feel the ghosts. Makes my skin tingle." She did a little itchy ass-dance in the front seat.

I thought she was being overly optimistic. The way she'd been wallowing in that bed where Kandy and Harry had bumped uglies, I'd lay wager her crotch was well on its way to becoming Knobby Waters' next great cootie castle.

Chapter Fourteen

B y the time we pulled into Dode's farmhouse yard, the thunder was loud as God's bowling alley. Rain splattered the windshield. The treetops whipped and scratched at the swollen bellies of the black clouds. Luckily Dode had a pair of automatic pole lights out by the barn. The storm had caused the electric eye sensor to flip the lights on. The lights sprayed a wide beam from the car to the house so we could see our way clear across the yard.

Dode was standing in overalls out on the front porch, waving our way. His rifle was leaned against the farmhouse door. He had a basket of what looked like flashlights sitting on the porch railing.

"Hot dog," said Veenie pointing toward the claw-like trees in the orchard. "See that storm? That's ghosts. They seen us coming." She unfolded an orange Hoosier Feedbag plastic shopping bag that she found on the floorboard of the Impala and stretched it over her head. She stretched it tight under her chin and made a little bow. "How do I look?"

"Fetching," I said.

In the backseat, Harry offered Kandy his suit jacket. He draped it up around her head and shoulders as they slid out of the car. She clung onto him big time as they slid across the yard toward the porch.

I pulled on my son Eddie's old green 4-H windbreaker, which I kept in the car for emergencies, and puckered the hood up around my ears. Veenie and I burst out of the Impala and dashed for the front porch. Rain spattered my glasses, but I figured they could use a good cleaning.

"Whoa boy, some storm, eh?" said Dode. His eyes were shining in the dark. He had his thumbs hooked under the apron on his bib overalls. "Bet the ghosts like this, eh?" Dode eyed us. "This here the séance lady?" He nodded toward Kandy.

Kandy stepped out from under Harry's jacket and shook her red locks. She finger-fluffed her hair before offering her ringed fingers to Dode. "Kandy Huggins," she said, "from the Henry Huggins bunch down around Scottsburg. I'm psychic. Got called up here by your ghost." Her bracelets jangled as they shook hands.

Dode's eyes widened. "For real? I mean I heard tell people could talk to spirits. My mother's people had the power. Course people today don't believe in such stuff, but I know darn certain what I saw."

Veenie asked Dode if he'd seen any ghosts the last few days.

He shook his head. "Not since you took that lady skeleton out of here. Not a snort. Not a peep. It's like they all died." He laughed nervously at his own joke.

Kandy assured us that silence was normal. "They're gathering energy. Waiting for us to call 'em home." She closed her eyes and felt the wet air with the palms of her hands. She wandered around the porch feeling the air like it was a thick wall. She stumbled on some uneven porch boards but recovered, clutching onto Harry. She shut her eyes and started in circles again, her hands held up high like a revival preacher.

Dode poked a piece of chaw into the pocket of his left jaw and sucked quietly. He followed Kandy's every move, mesmerized.

Kandy stopped twirling in circles and stared cross the yard and through the light to the shadowy outline of the Wyatt mansion. "We need to set up our séance over where you found the body. Over yonder. That the house?"

Dode nodded. "But the sheriff, he came by yesterday, taped it all up. Said nobody should be messing around over there. It's against the law. Said it was especially against the law if any old ladies showed up to snoop around."

Kandy rolled her eyes. She adjusted her bracelets. "They always do that. Cops. They don't understand spirits at all."

Harry made a little squeaky sound. "I dunno, sugar. I got a license to protect. Trespassing could get me in a heap of trouble, baby."

Kandy took him by the crook of his arm. She whispered into his ear like he was a small boy. "You aren't afraid of a little trouble are you, Harry?"

"I dunno." He shuffled his feet.

"Horse patootie," said Veenie. "The sheriff had his chance at this case. He all but threw it at us. We aren't hurting nothing."

Kandy tossed in her two cents. "Heck, it's Alta's house. She invited us. If you look at it that way, and that's the way any sane body would see the thing, it ain't even illegal trespassing. We're just going to visit a spell, like she asked."

While we were standing around debating breaking and entering and a litany of other possible felonies, a pair of truck lights swung up the road. The rain was thick enough we couldn't quite see who was coming. The lights bounced as the truck came closer over the rutted road. A white pickup, an older Ford F-150 with a cab on back, swung in and parked next to the Impala. A guy wearing a white baseball hat got out and strode across the yard toward the porch. He was wearing a pocket T-shirt with a red IU zip hoodie. He didn't seem bothered by the rain, which we could see spilling off the bill of his cap.

Dode stared at the guy as he grabbed the rail and hopped up the slippery steps to the porch. "Lord, Jesus!" he whistled.

To be honest, the guy did look like Jesus, long wavy brown hair. Blue eyes. Nice smile. In his thirties. His jeans were ripped at both knees. Took me a minute to realize it wasn't Jesus, but Randy Ollis standing there in the rain.

"Howdy," Randy said as he put out his hand toward Dode. He smiled at me and Veenie. "'Member me?"

"Sure do," said Veenie.

"Heard down at Pokey's you ladies were having a séance. Reckoned I'd drop by and see what my next of kin had to say. Brought company too." Randy turned and motioned for someone in the truck to roll down the window.

The window cranked down slowly. Darnell Zikes stuck his head out. His pigtails tossed a little in the wind. He had a yellow paisley bandana tied up on top of his head like a biker's do-rag. He waved our way with both pudgy hands.

"Met Darnell there at Pokey's. Told me he's staying with you ladies a couple of days. Told me about the séance tonight. Said he'd never seen a ghost, but sure would like to see one up close."

Darnell hopped out of the truck. He waddled as fast as he could in his Dr. Scholl's sliders toward the cover of the porch. He was wearing the same clothes as the night before. Blue-and-white plaid pedal pushers and a black wife beater T-shirt that read, "Save a horse. Ride a redneck."

"Okay if I join the party?" he asked as he shook his wet head like a dog drying off. His lazy eye meandered over the lot of us. "I mean, man this may be my only chance to do some ghost busting."

He introduced himself all around.

Dode said, "I like your eye." He pointed to Darnell's lazy eye. "How you get it to do that?"

"Born that way. My mama was the same."

Dode cocked his head. "You see sideways?"

"Nah. I see normal. It's just cosmetic. Doctors said I could get it fixed. Lazy muscle. The girls seem to like it. Makes me memorable."

Dode nodded. "It's right handsome. I'd probably keep it too."

Darnell stopped pumping hands when he got to Kandy. "You look mighty familiar. We met?" He squinted at her in the low light of the porch.

"Never," Kandy said.

"You sure?"

Kandy's lips tightened. "Very sure."

"All righty then. Say, where are them ghosts? We came to see them ghosts. They over there?" He pointed toward the mansion. "Cause that looks like a haunted house if ever I saw one."

Without waiting for an answer, Darnell jumped off the porch and ambled toward the orchard, headed toward the mansion. The rain had slowed to a trickle. He slid a little in the tall wet grass, looking back only once to urge us to follow him.

Dode handed the rest of us flashlights. We set off into the darkness of the apple orchard like a group of vigilantes in search of Frankenstein's monster.

Chapter Fifteen

Kandy didn't bring any special equipment for dialing up the dead.

That disappointed Veenie.

"We're lucky we got this here electrical storm. That'll do the trick," said Kandy as she wandered around the mansion's living room. "We don't need no fancy doohickeys or gadgets. Those are for the amateurs. If the Lord God gave you the gift, you don't have to lay out any fancy bait for the ghosts. They come screaming at you, eager for a chat. Some days I'll be driving peacefully down a gravel road at dark listening to some Shania Twain, and boom! I'll pass a graveyard. Next you know I'll have two or three of 'em crowding up next to me in the front seat of the Hyundai arguing about the weather."

Veenie's eyes widened. "Is it because you got a special electrical current running through you?"

"Yeah. Something like that," said Kandy. She ground out the cigarette she'd been smoking with the toe of her high heel.

Dode had taken the basket of flashlights and turned them all on. He'd placed them strategically around the room so we could see where to walk. One sat atop the fireplace mantle. A pair was sitting on their butts in far corners shining light up so the beams hit the spidery tin ceiling and fell back down in a pool around the room. Outside, the rain had died back, but the wind was whistling and creaking and thumping things around to beat the band. The place smelled like moldy baby diapers.

Not as many spider webs though. I guess the forensics team had cleared a lot of them away collecting scene samples.

Randy was taking little baby steps around the room, taking it all in. He was hugging the wall with his back. He seemed a little uneasy. "Whoa! Creepy. Can't believe my family once owned this place. Too bad they let it all rot. You'd think the government would have sold the place or done something with it all these years." He stopped in front of a flashlight beam. With his hair all loose and frizzy from his baseball cap and his arms outstretched, he looked like Jesus just dropped down for a visit. Kind of a comforting thought given all Veenie's talk about ghosts and demons.

Harry was sticking close to me. A little too close, in fact. I could smell his Brute aftershave. That stuff belonged on the deceased, as far as I was concerned. Harry was shaking a little too. He kept knocking into me. I reckoned he did believe in ghosts after all.

Darnell had disappeared. Either he had chickened out, or he was outside on the back porch taking a leak or toking. Or he was off hoping to find a snack in the kitchen. Or maybe he left because he forgot why he was there in the first place. Stoners were like that. Fidgety.

The room was draped in yellow police tape. Veenie had rolled up most of it and was wearing it around her body like a stripper's scarf. The rocking chair where we found the skeleton was still there, turned back upright.

Kandy pointed at the rocker. "That's where she died. I can feel it." Kandy closed her eyes and circled the rocker. She took hold of the back of the rocker and threw her head back. Her red curls bounced and her earrings shook.

Veenie asked what we should do to help.

Kandy sat down in the rocking chair. It creaked an awful lot. "You all make a circle around me. Hold hands. I'm going to start calling the ghost of Alta Iona. If you hold hands, it will create a positive electrical charge. She'll know you're friendly."

Veenie grabbed my right hand. Harry grabbed the other. Randy stepped up and connected to Harry. Dode completed the circle by hooking up between Randy and Veenie.

Kandy began to moan. Then she started talking in what sounded to me like pig Latin nonsense. "Oka nojenna mimi, grantis, greatus, oh spiritus, we come as friends."

A crack of lightning made us all jump.

Veenie yelled, "Alta Iona. It's me. Veenie. Lavinia Goens. Remember me? I helped lug you out of here. Since then I learned what that rascal Jedidiah did to you. Knocking you up and all."

Kandy opened her eyes. "You better let me handle this, Veenie. Once we get her dialed up, you can jump in with both feet, but it might take her awhile to feel safe."

Kandy started in with the pig Latin again.

I felt Veenie all jumpy, holding my hand. Keeping her trap shut was not her greatest talent. She was doing a little shuffle dance, like a kid who had to pee.

Kandy started humming and singing. She leaned into the rocking chair, and it began to creak and pick up speed. It sounded like it might bust apart any minute. Some dust and dirt got up my nose, and I started sneezing. Veenie followed suit.

Kandy started yapping in tongues again, and her voice grew huskier, gravelly, a bit like Linda Blair in *The Exorcist*. Now it was me who felt my bladder might give.

Harry's hand was shaking and sweating at the same time. I felt like I was holding a wet fish in my hand and that fish had started flopping, hoping to slip away. The smell of Brute was getting stronger.

Kandy was talking pig Latin so loudly she was practically shouting now. Her eyes were open, and her head was rolling around. I reckoned she must not have spinal arthritis because I did, and nothing swiveled that freely on me anymore. The voice coming out of Kandy's mouth screamed, "He killed me!"

"Who?" screamed Veenie in return. She was all spit and fire now. Jumping around on tiptoe, jerking me around with her. It was like dancing with a Holy Roller on revival day. "Who killed you, Alta? Who?"

The voice grumbled and rumbled and spat. She did not seem like a very happy ghost. "My husband. Jedidiah! He fed me poison, like a rat."

Veenie was all in now. "Why'd he do that?"

"He was mean as snake spit, plus he hated that baby."

"Myrtle Mae?"

The voice wailed. "My baby! My precious little baby!"

We were all feeling a little knock-kneed by then. I could see Dode across from me. If his eyes got any wider, they were going to pop out of his head like hard boiled eggs. I could see his legs shaking inside the wide legs of his overalls.

Veenie asked the voice, "But Jedidiah left town. How'd he know you were knocked up?"

"He came back."

"To get you and the baby?"

"To get the gold."

"Gold," Veenie screamed. "What gold?"

"The bank gold. I hid it from him."

Everything went a little quiet then. The voice disappeared, and in its place on the far wall was a womanly ghost dancing along the torn wallpaper. She floated. We couldn't see her feet. The long dress she was wearing, or robes, we couldn't tell because there were no details, only shadow and outline, billowed over her feet. She floated around on the wall like a bright shadow. She jerked around like an insect before fading completely away.

Veenie lunged for the wall. "Come back! What about the gold?"

Kandy groaned, sounding like Kandy again. Her neck snapped up, and she looked around like she wasn't sure what was going on. "Did she appear?" she asked.

"Yep," I said. "We got an awful eyeful."

Dode sniffled and stuffed a big plug of tobacco into his jaw. "Never seen nothing like that in all my born days. God damned, that was scary." Tobacco juice drizzled down his chin. "Better than Halloween."

Harry was white as a puddle of Elmer's Glue.

Randy was speechless, his mouth hanging open.

Darnell shuffled into the room. He was toking on a joint held in a roach clip. The clip had a couple of tiny feathers and a dream catcher dangling from it. His eyes were bloodshot. He'd peeled back his wet yellow do-rag. His hair stood out like a Brillo pad. One of his pigtails was unraveling. "I went to take a leak. Did I miss anything?"

Veenie asked Kandy if she could call back Alta Iona. "We need to know about that gold," she said.

Kandy stood up and cracked her back. "What gold?"

Veenie danced in circles over by the wall where Alta had swung around. "Alta said Jedidiah killed her. Came back for the gold."

Kandy looked confused. "What gold?" she repeated.

Randy stepped forward. He'd zipped up his red hoodie and was shivering a little. "My grandpa Ollis always said there was gold buried out here. We thought he was a little batty. His brain and tongue were both a little loose-jointed, runs in the family."

I spoke up. "Well the bank records Queet showed us at the library detailed thousands missing when they audited the bank after Jedidiah rowed out of town."

Veenie confirmed that. "That's right. And nobody knows what happened to old Jedidiah and that money. He could have come back after the flood. Maybe he hid the cash money here at the house. The flood came along, and whoosh, it was a perfect time to disappear."

I asked Randy if his granddad ever said anything specific about the money. "How much? Where was it hidden?"

Veenie wanted to know if Randy had ever seen a treasure map.

"Oh heck," said Randy, as he swept the Jesus hair out of his eyes. "All the papers I had I left at the library. I never heard tell of a treasure map. Just a lot of nonsense about how we was still rich, we just had to find the darn money."

I asked Kandy if she remembered any of the séance.

She lit a cigarette. "Gosh, sorry, no. My brain gets turned off once a spirit gets into me."

Veenie protested. "We need to chat some more with Alta. About the gold and all."

Kandy shook her curls. "Can't dial in more than once a night. Heck, now that she said her piece, she probably got sucked up into the Holy Hereafter. Her spirit may have gone on for good."

Kandy looked at Harry, who looked like a stick of chalk wearing a rumpled suit. "You got my money, sugar?" She held out her hand and wiggled her fingers. The light from the flashlights caught the fake jewels in her rings and sent little rainbows flashing onto the tin ceiling.

Harry fumbled in his trouser pockets. He pulled out a wad of money with a rubber band around it. His hand shook when he handed the roll to Kandy.

"Thanks," Kandy said, as she tucked the wad into her little shoulder purse. "We could try again. Wait a couple of days. But I can't be making no promises. You'd have to pay up front.

Take your chances. You want me to take another go at it, Dode?"

Dode cleared his throat. "Oh boy. Gosh darn it. Yep. I'd sure pay to see that again. She seemed pretty pissed. Had her dander up, all righty."

"Oh man!" whined Darnell. "You all got to see a real live ghost? Why didn't you wait on me? I was gone just a minute. Nature called." His stray eye stared at Kandy accusatively.

Or maybe it was my imagination.

Chapter Sixteen

I kicked off my rain-soaked shoes and belly flopped onto my bed. And I didn't wake up until after dawn. Sassy Sue Ann Smith, our boarder, woke me up slamming pots and pans in the kitchen.

"Lord, God, Almighty, what are you doing?" I asked Sassy as I slid past her to put on a pot of coffee. I had a sour stomach. All that ghost talk and spirit dancing had given me nightmares. At one point, I'd shot up in bed. I was clutching the sheets over a dream that featured a giant whiskered catfish swallowing me whole. Boots had been in that one. He was either Noah or Jonah. One of those Biblical guys with a white beard. I was hoping some Cheerios might settle my stomach.

Sassy had her back to me. She was mashing buttons on the microwave. I could tell it was her from the cloud of White Shoulders perfume. Two ripped cartons of Jimmie Dean breakfast sausages and eggs and biscuits were tossed on top of the stove. A loaf of white bread was torn open. The air near the toaster smelled like a smoldering campfire. Several pieces of scraped toast were piled atop each other on a coffee saucer. Sassy, per usual, was falling short in the homemaking department.

Sassy whirled around. She was wearing a red, knee-length lingerie jacket with a black boa collar. She wore a black lace bustier under that. Her blonde hair was teased up so high it looked like the leaning tower of Pisa, if those Italians had thought to make it out of hay. She'd stuck in a butterfly pin here and there in an effort to keep it upright. Her face was painted with lips as large and red as slices of watermelon. The pink rouge on her cheeks looked like war paint. Her mascara had seeped into her crow's feet, giving her more of a vulture claw look. "Making breakfast, sugar. I got a new man in my room."

"Course you do." Sassy had always been a swinger.

"Can you make us some of that good pot coffee?" she purred.

"Making a whole pot."

I trudged to the refrigerator and knocked around looking for a carton of milk. I grabbed a box of Cheerios and a bowl from the cabinet.

Sassy started humming a show tune. I think it was "Me and My Man."

The microwave beeped. Sassy sprung open the door. She slipped on an oven glove and pulled out two plastic trays of sausage, and biscuits and gravy, and an egg mash-up. She grabbed a giant serving spoon and used it to scoop the mess onto a pair of blue-and-white CorningWare plates. She slapped a slice of blackened toast on top of each volcano of food. She stood back and admired her work.

"This look appetizing?" she asked, her lips pursed.

Veenie strolled into the kitchen. "Where'd you get that two-bit getup?"

"Frederick's of Hollywood, Little Dash of Class collection." Sassy twirled once so we could get an eyeful. You could tell that sixty years ago she'd been a star pupil at the Twinkle Toes Tap & Twirl dance studio.

Veenie snatched a piece of Sassy's sausage. She tossed it in the air, then caught it in her mouth like dog kibble. She squeezed into a chair at the table next to me. "That Jimmy Dean makes some tasty meat. Ought to make fancy deserts. I bet he'd make a badass sausage cake with gravy buttercream frosting. I ought to call him up. He'd make a killing on sausage cakes with buttercream frosting. Put some bacon in there. Make them bacon layer cakes. I'd buy that stuff in bulk at the Costco."

I poured us all some coffee. "Sassy has a man in her room."

"Is he handcuffed to anything?" asked Veenie.

Sassy made a face. "I'll have you know he's a southern gentleman. From the city. Louisville. The VFW was having a private party on the *Belle of Louisville*. He asked me for a dance."

The *Belle of Louisville* was a restored Civil War-era paddle boat and floating buffet and full-service bar that docked in Louisville and cruised the Ohio River. Lots of southern Indiana clubs rented it out for dances and big shindigs.

Veenie stole another piece of sausage. "We talking the dance with no pants?"

"Lavinia, I'll have you know he drove me all the way back up here after he bought me a surf and turf dinner. This was a proper date, and I've just been saying thank you." Sassy teetered down the hall with her breakfast tray to the privacy of her own room. Whoever she was dating, I reckoned she wasn't ready to introduce us to him. Probably a wise move given that not everyone took to Veenie right away.

Veenie clicked on her iPad. "Didn't want to wake you up, RJ."

"Didn't stop you night before last." I gulped hot black coffee until my eyes sprang open.

"Think I found Junior's missing Harley." She slid her iPad toward me. It was opened to a page on Craigslist. There was a photo of a Harley for sale. It was an older, mysterious red Street 750 like Junior's. Not an expensive bike, nor a very powerful bike, but then Junior wasn't all that much of a street stud. The bike was priced to move. Only three thousand. Cash. The "cash" part had a lot of exclamation points after it. There was an email address but no more information. The ad had been posted only an hour ago.

"What makes you think that's Junior's bike? Probably tons of bikes like that in Southern Indiana." I sucked down more coffee.

"Lookie," said Veenie. She squashed her fat fingers on the screen and blew it up a little.

I could see what she was talking about. In the extreme right of the photo you could see the tip of a covered bridge. No doubt about it, it was the Knobby Waters covered bridge. The seller was local.

Veenie shot an email to the Craigslist Harley seller and got an almost immediate ping back. The seller said we could see the bike that afternoon. He gave the covered bridge as the rendezvous point. Reiterated that it was a cash deal. No guarantees. No questions. No bickering.

Veenie, who was using the screen name Hog Mama, typed back, "No problem, man."

"Who you reckon stole Junior's bike?" Veenie asked me.

I shrugged. "Whoever took it is must be after fast cash. Probably in debt for child support."

"Well that leaves most of the male population of Knobby Waters in the running."

I heard a clomping up the cellar stairs, and Fergie Junior popped through the door. He was wearing an oversized Grateful Dead T-shirt and a pair of tighty-whities. He had on his John Lennon glasses and a pair of floppy, red flannel house slippers.

Veenie eyed him as he headed toward the refrigerator. "What are you doing above ground? It's daylight."

Junior murmured as he rummaged in the refrigerator. He pulled out a PBR and popped the tab. His reddish moustache was foamy when he pulled the can away. "Darnell woke me up.

Wha'did'y'all do to him last night? He was freaked. Came home all muddy about an hour ago, ranting about ghosts."

"An hour ago?" I asked. "You sure?" Darnell had ridden back home from Dode's with us, but that had been several hours ago.

"Sure, I'm sure." Junior scraped up a kitchen chair and plopped into the seat. He slurped more beer. He poured a handful of Cheerios out of the box and slurped those down with a beer chaser. "I was just finishing a recording for the dudes in Indianapolis. He's passed out on the futon downstairs. I think he might be stoned."

Veenie said we hadn't done anything to Darnell. "He was at the séance, but he went to take a leak. Missed the ghost."

"Ghosts, yeah, right," Junior chortled. "And what have you two been smoking?"

Veenie stuck her teeth out at Junior.

"Gross, Ma." Junior snatched the box of Cheerios and lumbered back down the stairs.

I asked Veenie if maybe we should have told Junior about his Harley and how we were going to fetch it for him.

"Nah," she said.

"Why not?"

"'Cause he'll want to ride along, and I'm not in the mood for his chatter. I love that boy, you know I do, but gosh darn, some days he so reminds me of his daddy. And when that happens, I just want to smack him right up the side of the head."

I could definitely see her point.

Chapter Seventeen

When we arrived under the covered bridge an hour later, Junior's Harley was sitting in a sunny spot with a handwritten "4 Sale" sign hung over the handlebars. It looked fine, red and shiny like an apple. Behind the Harley, a footpath led down through the weeds to the muddy river's edge. We could see the better part of a car parked down by the river. Someone looked to be camping, which wasn't odd. The odd part was the car. It was a purple Gremlin with white stripes. I hadn't seen one of those since the seventies when the high school Spanish teacher from Indiana State had tooled around town in one the same color.

The thing looked like a sawed-off station wagon. Or a clown car. Whoever rode in the back seat had to ride with their knees poked into their chest. All through the seventies, people like me suffered to high heaven in the name of better gas mileage. Always felt to me like I was rattling around strapped to a roller skate. I had a second cousin who had a wreck playing chicken in a Gremlin out on Highway 50 near Crane Hill. They power-washed what was left of him off the asphalt.

The hatchback on this one was open. A white canvas tent had been puckered around the back. A clothesline was strung between two trees with a pair of T-shirts and some man's boxer underpants fluttering on it. A cold campfire lay at the side of the Gremlin.

Veenie squinted as we got out of the Impala. "That a Gremlin?"

"Appears to be."

"Always thought them cars were so dang cute."

"You're short. And trendy. You would."

A boy popped out of the weeds by the Gremlin. He was riding a rusty girl's banana seat bicycle a size too big for him. The seat was sparkly and spotted pink. I recognized the little fellow as Pooter Johnson. He was maybe eleven years old and infamous as the up-and-coming entrepreneur of Knobby Waters. Every Monday he hung out in the parking lot outside the Hoosier Feedbag selling bags of produce that fell from the harvest trucks. He was wearing dark aviator sunglasses with fat chrome rims, cutoff jean shorts, and no shirt. His hair, the color of a field mouse, was home buzzed and full of scalp nicks. He spun to a stop in the sand in front of us, almost popping the Velcro closures on his yellow high-tops.

Veenie whispered to me, "I think he thinks he's Tom Cruise in *Top Gun.*"

I was thinking more like Pooter was stuck with his sister's hand-me-down bicycle and maybe sunglasses too. He had four older sisters, two which were famous for sitting on the steps out in front of Pokey's, sucking on pop bottles. Their mom, who was a kind and decent woman and head waitress at the Roadkill Café, was constantly running around town trying to round up him and his sisters, keep them all headed in some direction other than prison, where their daddy had an executive timeshare.

"You got to admire that little fart's hustle," said Veenie as Pooter hopped off the bike and tossed it in the weeds. "Having to ride around town with a big, sparkly pink banana between his legs, a lot of little boys would just lay down and cry."

Pooter spat at the sand as he sauntered toward us. "One of you Hog Mama?"

"She is," I pointed to Veenie.

"Yeah, that's me," said Veenie. "That there the hog you're selling?"

"Depends. You got cash money?"

"Depends. You got a pink slip?"

He spat again. "That some kind of remark about my bicycle or my manhood?"

"No," I said. "A pink slip is an ownership slip. When you sell a vehicle, you sign the slip over to the buyer, so we can register it for a new license plate."

"The hog ain't mine. I'm just the sales agent." He strolled around the motorbike. "It appears it ain't got no plates."

"Why not?" I asked.

"They plum fell off, I reckon." He crossed his arms.

I was having a hard time seeing Pooter climb onto and navigate a Harley, and I'd never known him to steal anything outright. He was more of an honest opportunist, trying to make a buck as best he could. His claim that he was the sales agent struck me as about right. "That your camp down yonder?" I asked.

He glanced over his shoulder. "Why you asking?"

"Haven't seen a Gremlin like that in a long time. Maybe we want to buy that too."

Pooter squinted at me. "It ain't for sale. Look, Granny, I'm trying to make a living. You want to buy this hog or not? Cause, like, I got another guy coming. Maybe two or three. This ain't the Big Lots. We don't do layaway."

Of course, we didn't have three thousand dollars. We had maybe three dollars in chump change between us in the Impala's ashtray. I thought for a moment. "Okay, look, we're going to get the cash. But we got to drive back to town. The bank. Hit the ATM. It'll take us about twenty minutes. OK?"

Veenie looked at me like I was crazy.

"Come on, Hog Mama." I pulled on her sleeve. "Let's get the dough."

Veenie followed me back to the Impala.

I started the car. It smoked like a chimney.

Pooter yelled after us. "Hey, Granny, your car's on fire! You might want to have a mechanic take a look at that!"

I waved at him out the window as I cut a donut and headed toward town. A hundred feet down the road, I cut down the pull-off to the Moon Glo Motor Lodge. I idled in the pull-off for a while.

"What in the high heavens are you doing?" asked Veenie. "We don't have three thousand dollars, and you *know* that's Junior's bike."

"I have a notion whoever stole that bike is camping in that Gremlin."

"So?"

"So we got to sneak back. Take a look at that campsite."

I didn't have to say that again. Veenie popped out of the Impala and started through the weeds the back way along the riverbank to the Gremlin camp.

The campfire at the Gremlin site was cold, filled with charred driftwood. There was a stinking pile of fish heads close to the fire pit. Green flies buzzed over the pile in a cloud. The only other thing moving was the dancing men's underpants in the breeze from the river. The camper had rigged up a rope and pulley in the sycamore trees. A large, black plastic garbage bag hung in a ball from a high tree limb. The camper had hoisted up his dry food store to keep the varmints from stealing it. A bobcat had been sighted slinking around the river bottoms. Anybody with any sense and camping experience would have protected the dry food.

The Gremlin was unlocked. Veenie slid into the front seat, passenger's side, and popped open the glove compartment.

"What's in there?" I asked. "A registration?"

"Nah," she said. She pulled her hands out of the glove compartment. They were filled with crumpled tissues, a wad of disposable blue plastic gloves, and a book of paper matches from Pokey's. "Just junk. And a harmonica." The harmonica was nice, an old one made of silver and copper.

I leaned into the car. It smelled like an ashtray, and it was filthy. Crushed beer cans. Cigarette and doobie butts. A bait and tackle box. Couple of cheap Zebco fishing poles and reels. A fishing net. Candy bar wrappers. Dirty clothes. And lots of nudie magazines. *Jugs*, *Really Big Jugs*, and *Farm Girls with Jugs*.

"I think he has a type," I said to Veenie.

The ripped back seat had been flipped down. An air mattress took up the back. Mountains of blankets and ratty old quilts were heaped on top of the mattress. The tent was puckered out over that.

Veenie eyed the mess. "Who you reckon lives here?"

"Not Martha Stewart," I said as I held up an unbelievably dirty athletic sock.

"Hey," called Veenie from outside the car. "Lookie here at this."

I crawled out of the Gremlin and walked over to the shady side of the car next to the river. Several empty plastic ice bags lay in the mud with the words "Moon Glo Motor Lodge" printed in blue on the side. These were scattered alongside a wheeled, blue plastic cooler. I was a little afraid to open the cooler.

Veenie, on the other hand, flipped it right open.

"What's in there?"

Veenie thrust her hands into an icy slush and held up a dripping white plastic bag. The label on the side read, "Mystery Meat."

"Think we found Pokey's thief," Veenie said.

Just then Pooter Johnson popped up in the weeds at the edge of the campsite. "Hey! Get out of there!" he cried. "You don't want to be messing with this stuff. You old ladies crazy, or what?"

Veenie sauntered up to Pooter. "We came back with the dough, but you were gone."

"No way. I been here waiting for you. I was up there waiting for you. Been right here the whole time."

"Well, we got the dough. But first we want a test drive. How we know that hog runs?"

Pooter looked suspicious.

Veenie ignored him and traipsed up the path toward the Harley.

Pooter raced after her.

I did the same.

She started inspecting the bike. "I'd be buying this here bike for my boyfriend. It run good?"

"Course it does. I don't sell no junk."

"Start it up," said Veenie.

"Show me the money," said Pooter.

"Look, snot nose, I'm old, and it makes me cranky. You don't want to get your ass whooped, you start up that hog so I can see it run, or else I'm calling your mama and telling her where you are and what you're doing."

Pooter sulked. "Okay, keep your giant granny panties on."

He mounted the bike and keyed it. It roared to life. He wrestled the kick down and left it running. It did run smoothly, but then Junior was fussy about his ride.

Veenie straddled the bike. She practically had to run and jump to make the mount. For a minute, I thought the whole thing was going to crash down on her, but next we both knew she was spinning out of the sand. She roared out and onto the gravel road, the bike lurching and screaming. She looked like a fat kewpie doll turned Evil Knievel.

"What the heck!" called Pooter as he ran after her. "Gosh darn it! Gosh darn it to hell!" He stomped in the sand. "You come back here! Hey!" he said, turning red-faced to me. "Your lady friend stole my hog!"

"Oh hey, you want me to call the police and report it?"

Pooter turned redder and sputtered more.

I left him like that and went smoking toward town after Veenie, but not before I memorized the license plate on the Gremlin and texted Boots to look up the car owner's registration for me.

Chapter Eighteen

When I swung the Impala into my driveway, the Harley was leaning up against the house by the back cellar door, but there was no sign of Veenie. I was relieved to see that she'd made it home. Crazy old coot. One of these days she was going to get herself into some serious trouble. I already had the bail money set aside.

Sassy was sitting in the porch swing. A white-haired gentleman with a little goatee sat next to her. Gratefully, they were both dressed. With Sassy, attire could be an uncertain item. After being born and raised in Knobby Waters, she'd run away and lived most of her adult life with swingers out in California.

Sassy and her man friend were swinging back and forth, surrounded by pots of red geraniums and purple petunias. She waved as I loped up the sidewalk. "What's Veenie doing riding Junior's bike? Thought she lost her license?"

"She did." I limped up onto the porch, my bad knee a little achy. The limestone steps were steep and wide. And my right knee was bothering me from scrambling around in the Gremlin. I grabbed the rusted iron railing and heaved myself up onto the concrete porch. "She did lose her license, but she was in a hurry today, and I wasn't driving fast enough, I reckon."

The man on the porch swing stood up and introduced himself. "Melvin Beal," he said. "Pleased to meet you." He extended a well-manicured hand.

"Likewise," I said. "Ruby Jane Waskom, but most folks just call me RJ, so feel free."

"I'm from around Louisville. Met this precious, little flower of a lady down on the *Belle*." He rolled a shoulder toward Sassy, who beamed like a hunter who'd just dragged home a prized catch. And I had to admit Melvin did look pretty darn good compared to most of the prey Sassy hog-tied and brought home.

He was rail thin, wearing fussy, gray dress slacks and a white turtleneck that went well with his tidy goatee. His thin, white hair was plastered in place and he was wearing thick-rimmed glasses. His feet were clad in Florsheim tasseled loafers that were spit polished. He was wearing an expensive gold-link watch and smelled like English Leather. He had perfect teeth that didn't chatter on their own or lisp. Dental implants, I reckoned. He smelled like a Southern gentleman.

He said he'd been reading about the ghost case and was fascinated. "Just fascinated."

"Being a PI does keep me and Veenie busy," I said.

"And ghost busting," he said. "My, oh my. We got a lot of ghosts down South. Never seen one myself, though. Once, when I was a freshman at Ole Miss, after a little too much moonshine, I did see some strange things. But I think that was the liquor." He chuckled a little.

I sat down in the rocking chair closest to Melvin.

Melvin returned to his seat next to Sassy on the porch swing.

Sassy swung an arm around him. "Melvin here is officially retired, but he still drives around and does a bit of business. Sells liquor to the high-class joints."

"I sure do," said Melvin. "Play the ponies a bit too. You ladies ever go to the track? Churchill Downs?"

Sassy took hold of that suggestion. "I'd love to go the track with you."

"Well, ok, sweet pea," he said. "Course I'll be taking you."
He patted her hand.

Sassy smooched his cheek.

Oh boy. I hoped the neighbors weren't watching. Mrs.
Thelma Nierman, across the way, was ninety-one years old,
head of the Baptist Ladies' Auxiliary, and pretty strict about
keeping my porch G-rated. She was always on me about
making Junior wear pants when he came out on the porch to
retrieve the mail. She knew better than to get after Veenie, who
always spat back. I reckoned she thought if she cawed at me
enough I'd whip Veenie into shape.

Melvin wanted to know about the ghosts.

I told him about the séance.

He seemed intrigued but a hair dubious. "You really of the
mind that place is haunted?"

"The show I saw was pretty convincing." I was still having
nightmares about that floating ghost on the wall. And Dode
was sure enough sold on the idea, so much so he'd already given
permission for us to book Kandy for a second séance.

Melvin stroked his goatee. "But surely you know people
like this, this ..."

"Kandy Huggins," I suggested.

"Yes, people like her, they make their living duping people
using little more than old carnival tricks."

"Sure, I know that, but what is it Dode's been seeing in the
apple orchard?"

"You ever see what he saw?"

"Gosh no. Veenie and I poked around that orchard before
Kandy ever got involved, but all we saw was spiders and gopher
holes."

"You searched the whole house?"

"Nah. Never got a chance. You think we should?"

"I certainly would."

My mind chewed on that idea for a spell. "Sheriff has it roped off." I thought of Boots's warning that Veenie and I weren't supposed to go near the place now that it was a crime scene. Of course we'd already ignored that choice bit of advice.

As if on cue, Boots pulled up in his cruiser. He slid out and mashed his sheriff's hat on before strolling up the walk.

"Evenin' all," he said to me and Sassy and Melvin. He doffed his hat when he met Melvin. "New around these parts, aren't you?"

"From Louisville. I trade up this way. Sell liquor from time to time over at the French Lick resorts."

Sassy spoke up. "He's my beau."

"Darn tootin' I am, sweet pea," Melvin said, giving her another cheek peck.

"Well, glad to have you," said Boots. He slid his hat back on and eyed me. "I got that information you asked about, Ruby Jane." His eyes slid around the porch like maybe he wanted to talk in private.

"I was just fixing to make us some iced tea. Come on in. We can talk about it while I get some kitchen work done."

Sassy fluttered her fingers "bye" to us.

Melvin said, "Nice meeting you both. Hope to be a frequent visitor up this way."

Once inside the kitchen, Boots slid out a chair and sat down. "Word around town is that you and Lavinia went ghost hunting out at that mansion again."

Oh boy. "You want sugar or honey in your tea?" I asked Boots.

"Ruby Jane."

"Yes."

"Don't mess with me."

"I'm putting sugar in yours. Lemon too."

"Ruby Jane." He sounded gruff now.

"Oh for heaven's sake, course we went out there. Dode is our client. He hired us. You sent him to us. We took him off your hands. You ought to be grateful. So quit your bellyaching and drink your tea." I smacked the glass down in front of him.

He ignored the tea. "It's my job to uphold the law."

"Oh fiddlesticks. You ignore the law all the time. I've seen you fishing out of season. Hunting too."

He reddened. "This isn't me. The order to seal the crime scene came from the boys upstate. Might even involve the Feds."

I sat down. "The Feds? Why do they care about ghosts in some old, falling down house in the gosh-darn middle of nowhere?"

"Dunno. Not my job to ask questions of the muckety-mucks. Not yours either."

"We talking FBI?"

"Might be."

"You're joshing, right?"

He shrugged and sipped his tea. "I'm telling you that for once in your life, you ought to try listening to the voice of authority for just one itty-bitty second."

"And that voice just happens to be yours?"

After a couple of sips of tea, he spoke. "I got the name registered on that license plate you texted me."

"Who is it?"

"Registered to a Tab Slygo, over in Washington County. Salem."

"He got a record?"

"Not an arrest record. But he did report that car stolen, couple of weeks ago." Boots checked the notepad on his cell phone. "It's a Gremlin, right?"

I nodded.

"Boy those were butt-ugly cars," he said with a shake of his head. "First time I saw one of those cars I knew America was headed straight into the crapper."

Car-wise, I had to agree.

"Where'd you see this here stolen Gremlin? In town?"

I figured it couldn't hurt to come clean. "Saw it parked in a camp site, down under the covered bridge." I gave Boots the quick and dirty on Pooter Johnson and the stolen Harley and the stolen bags of mystery meat we'd found in the campsite cooler. "Whoever is driving that Gremlin is bad news."

"Camping overnight is illegal. That's a state landmark."

"Maybe you ought to investigate that instead of badgering us old ladies."

He stood up and mashed his hat onto his head. "You're only old on the outside, Ruby Jane. Inside, you're nine. Haven't changed a spit bit since grade school." He hesitated. "What would I be looking for if I were to arrest the driver of that Gremlin?"

"Isn't it enough that he stole that car?"

"Guess so. You sure snot-nosed Pooter Johnson isn't the mastermind behind all this?"

"Pooter Johnson isn't the mastermind of anything. If snot were dynamite, that boy couldn't blow his own brains out."

That got a chuckle out of Boots. He headed toward the screen door but turned when his hand hit the door. "No more séances. You hear?"

"I hear."

Once Boots was out the door I glanced at my cell, which had been vibrating to beat the band. Veenie had texted me that she was working on getting the second séance set up.

I wanted to yell after Boots that I'd heard what he said ... and that I intended to ignore him. I decided what the hey, a town this small he'd know what I was up to before I did. Heck, the *Hoosier Squealer* had probably already posted the whole thing online, and it hadn't even happened yet.

Chapter Nineteen

Dickie Freeman kept his word. He picked up the Impala for repairs and an inspection with a promise to return it within the week. I hated to see the Chevy go, but Dickie wasn't charging us one red cent. He'd even snagged us a replacement radiator from the junkyard at a senior discount.

The problem was Veenie and I had no wheels. Or so I thought. Veenie informed me otherwise. "Lookie what Dickie made us," she said. We were at the office catching up on paperwork. Veenie tugged me up by the hand. We went out on the sidewalk together.

"What in tarnation?" I said, when I saw what had Veenie so excited.

"It's a two-seater, go-kart," she beamed. "And lookie, it takes gasoline." She pointed to a gas tank that had been mounted on the chassis. "Got an engine and lights and a toot horn." She squeezed a bell horn. It sounded like a rhinoceros with a cold. The seats were molded plastic orange seats like the ones they had at the bus station. A roll bar protected the seat cage. There was a white wicker basket behind the two seats, big enough to haul around a couple of bags of groceries.

"It runs?" I asked. It wasn't the prettiest thing. It appeared to be welded from a hodgepodge of parts—part lawn mower, part bicycle, part dune buggy. All Veenie.

"Runs up to thirty miles per hour," she said proudly.

"Street legal?"

"Dickie said I don't need no license long as I stay off the highway."

That was good since Veenie had lost her license for mowing down a few too many parking meters. I always drove because I had a license, but also because Veenie drove like she was auditioning for the Indy 500. Danica Patrick had nothing on her. Except eyesight. Veenie couldn't see worth pig crap.

It was only six blocks from our house to work. Everything we needed was downtown. The Hoosier Feedbag for groceries. The bank, across the street from the office. Pokey's down the alley. The Road Kill Café was only three blocks away. As long as it didn't rain, we could scoot around on Veenie's go-kart perfectly fine. Veenie hadn't wrecked the Harley, so surely she could handle this baby. Not like I had much choice. I wasn't about to take Junior's Harley anywhere. I'd never gotten the hang of driving a motorbike. My only other transportation option was my grown son Eddie, who lived in a repurposed Bunny Bread delivery truck. And at my age I refused to be delivered to anyone's doorstop like day-old bread.

"I reckon it will do." I was still inspecting the thing—it didn't seem to have any brakes—when Harry sauntered down the sidewalk.

"What in the Sam Hill is that?" He bent down and duck walked around the contraption.

"It's mine," said Veenie proudly.

"Don't doubt that," said Harry. "It looks like you. I mean, what's it for?"

"Driving."

"Show me," said Harry.

Veenie climbed in the driver's seat. She put on her red IU football helmet, the one she'd bought for ghost busting, and strapped it tight to her chin. She pulled the starter coil on the go-kart, and it backfired and spat like a lawn mower on its last leg. It rattled and rumbled. She released a lever. The thing shot out of the parking spot and down the street. Last we saw Veenie she was rolling on two wheels around the corner toward the library. We lost sight of her but could still hear her. She sounded like a giant wasp.

Boots drove around the corner. He pulled over and powered down his window. "What in the name of hell was that?" he asked, looking at me. He had been wearing his cop sunglasses but yanked them off so he could look me in the eye.

"What?" I asked.

"That thing. Just blew past me. Looked like Veenie was driving." He hitched a thumb over his shoulder.

"Oh that. Go-kart."

"She can't be driving that thing on the street."

"Why don't you talk to her about that?"

"She never listens."

Boy was that an understatement. "You need something?" I asked.

He slid over into a parking space and unfolded out of the cruiser. "I was just down at the covered bridge."

"You find the Gremlin?"

"No."

"It was there yesterday."

"Not today." He adjusted his gun belt. "Thought I'd go over to the Hoosier Feedbag. See if Pooter Johnson is set up in the back parking lot." Pooter was often there, selling leftover produce he bogarted after the fields had been gleaned. Last week he'd had some kick ass early asparagus. I'd bought some cheap right before old man Butler, who ran the Hoosier Feedbag produce department, had rolled in to close Pooter down.

"Let me know if you find out anything." I said as Harry and I headed back into the office.

I spent a dreary afternoon in the office with Harry catching up with the paperwork. Dode called about closing time and broke up the humdrum.

"They're back!" He sounded breathless.

"The ghosts?"

"Yep! Saw them swinging their big butts around about dawn this morning."

"In the house?"

"Nah, the orchard."

"Same as before?"

"Exact same. Been keeping my eye on the place. Just a few minutes ago heard some commotion over there."

"What kind of commotion?"

"Hard to say. Like cat-a-wailing. Big time."

Given how many stray cats lived around that mansion, I could see a hissy cat fight or two breaking out easy enough. "You want me to come out?"

"Sure would appreciate that. Bring that lady medium. They seemed to like her."

I wasn't sure "like" was the word I would have chosen, but whatever was going on in that mansion, Kandy seemed able to tease it out and into talking. Unfortunately Kandy wasn't booked yet. We were still waiting for her to feel the spirit.

I asked Harry if he'd give me a ride out to Dode's place.

He leaned back in his chair and tightened his tie, which he'd let go loose while doing the paperwork. "Thought the séance was later."

"It is, but Dode says the ghosts are back. Now."

"I dunno," said Harry. He looked a little white around the edges. His moustache tightened. He reached in his desk drawer and pulled out a gun and shoulder holster. He strapped it on before slipping into his jacket. He grabbed a handful of bullets from the desk drawer and stuffed them into his vest pocket.

"Thought you didn't believe in ghosts," I said as we locked up.

He mumbled something about me being old and half-crazy and how it was his sworn job to protect me.

Yeah. Like he was fooling me. I kept my pie hole closed and climbed into Harry's Toyota. It felt kind of nice to be riding shotgun again.

By the time we reached Dode's farmhouse it was tending toward dusk.

Dode was in his customary place on the porch, his rifle resting across his knees. He had a pitcher of well water on the table. A couple of stray cats sat on the porch rail. They ran when they saw me and Harry coming toward them.

"Any more action?" I asked as we climbed the steps.

He spat into a Mountain Dew can. "Nah. Quiet over there. Think they heard me calling you up."

"You ever see a light on in that house?" I asked.

"Nah. Just the orchard."

"Where exactly?" I asked. "Can you take us over. Point out the spot?"

"Sure can." Dode got up and straightened his back a bit. He offered us flashlights and then took off down the steps, climbing sideways like a crab. If that hip hurt him, he never complained. And it didn't seem to slow him down any once he got ambling along.

We stopped in the back of the orchard, close to the back porch of the mansion. There were still a few strands of yellow police tape fluttering in the apple trees close to the porch. The wind had kicked up. The house shutters were creaking a little.

"About here," said Dode. He stopped and ran his flashlight in a wide circle.

I clicked on my flashlight and walked toward the area Dode had highlighted. It was close to the house, behind the pile of boards and tin rubble, a place Veenie and I had not searched before.

Harry took a flashlight from Dode and swung his beam to the right of mine.

"What you looking for?" asked Dode. "Ghost slime?"

"Not sure," I confessed. "Anything odd, I reckon."

Harry yelled from the other side of the tree, "Dang it to hell!"

"What's wrong?" I asked, swinging my light his way.

"Gopher holes. All over the place. Twisted my ankle."

Dode and I walked over. We shone our lights onto the grass under Harry's feet.

"Not gophers," Dode said. "Nope. Not gophers."

"How can you tell?" asked Harry, who was a city boy.

"Look how big these here holes are." Dode dug a boot into a hole, and his booted foot disappeared up to his ankle. "And there ain't no tunnel between them."

I looked closer. He was right. There were a lot of holes, and they were big, but there were no little heaved up lines of dirt connecting them. Gophers tunneled close to the surface. All underground varmints did.

I asked Dode what he figured made the holes.

"I reckon it was ghosts," he said. He was over by the house now. There were a pile of old boards. Also, a pile of rusted tin sheets stacked a couple of feet high. He kicked a few things aside before dropping down on one knee to dig in the ground with his pocket knife. He uncovered a partially buried pair of shovels and a pair of large lights—camping lanterns that had high-intensity beams.

Harry drug the shovels and lights out of the pile. He brushed off one of the lights and flicked on a switch. The light beamed out over the orchard.

Dode's eyes lit up.

"That what you've been seeing at night, Dode?" I asked.

"Reckon it might be," he said.

Harry swung the light around the exterior of the house. Everything looked dark and sealed up tight. He moved the light across the ground and ran it over the trash pile. We could see some shoe prints over in the corner in the damp sand. We couldn't make out much in the way of the type or size of the shoe, though.

Harry grunted. He shoved his hat back on his head. "I don't think ghosts use high-beam flashlights."

"Or wear shoes," I said.

Chapter Twenty

Veenie spat bullets when I told her Harry and I had gone ghost hunting without her and found the high-beam lights, shovels, and shoe prints.

"Gosh, darn! You should have called me!"

"You *v-v-v-roomed* out in your go-kart. Where'd you go?"

"Library."

Veenie had just come into the living room. It was after dark, and she was carrying a couple of new Father Mackie romance books. I was curled up on the couch under an afghan watching *Perry Mason*. Paul had just gotten pistol-whipped. Della was busy saving his blonde beach boy ass. Boy, that Della always got things done. She should have had her own show.

"Don't think I ever saw this one," Veenie said as she plopped down in the La-Z-Boy and popped up the recliner stool.

"Course you have," I said. "You just forgot."

"I dunno. Maybe I got that early onset Alzheimey thing."

"It's not early," I said. "You're seventy-one."

Sassy sashayed into the room. "Trying to decide which dress to wear tonight. Melvin is taking me out to the Pawpaw County VFW banquet." She held up a reddish sequined number with a side-leg slit.

Veenie wrinkled her nose. "Don't wear that one. It'll make you look like a lumpy hot dog."

Sassy whipped out another one and held it up against her sternum. "This is my go-to, knock 'em dead dress." It was black with one shoulder and one long black sleeve. The other side was off-the-shoulder completely. It was white from the waist down and the skirt dropped to sweep the floor. The bottom was flared like a mermaid's tail. It was way too sophisticated for me. I never was much for getting gussied up.

Veenie studied the dress as Sassy twirled around the living room dancing with it. Sassy was like this. Always partying, even if there was no one else around.

"Yeah, that one," nodded Veenie. "It screams 'I'm such an airheaded I lost half my dress already.' Men get excited by that shit."

"Thanks girls," said Sassy. "You two staying in tonight?" She gathered both dresses in her arms.

I tucked the afghan under my chin. "I got a hot date later with the men of *Bonanza*."

Sassy shook her head. "You ought to date that sheriff. I hear tell he's sweet on you."

"I had a husband," I mumbled. That was true. I'd married Charlie "Whiskers" Waskom right out of high school, and we'd popped out two kids, Eddie and Joyce. Eddie still moped around Pawpaw County but my daughter Joyce, a social climber, had attended IU and moved over to Monroe County in Bloomington. She was married to Mr. Insurance of Southern Indiana, Rusty Krotch, a successful pot-bellied little guy from Atlanta with a hawkish face, who I'd always found a wee bit light in the loafers. He was one heck of an insurance salesman, though. My own husband, Charlie, had died suddenly when our kids were still in high school. He was a good man and a great daddy to our kids, but our marriage, in hindsight, had been a heap of work.

"Have another go at a husband," recommended Sassy. "I've had four. The more you do it, the better it gets. Don't you miss having a big old man hugging on you?"

"I don't miss having a big old man leaving his laundry all over the place."

Veenie asked me to toss her the bag of Cheetos. I complied, and she ripped right into it. "RJ ain't romantic like us," she mumbled at Sassy between cheese curls.

"Fiddlesticks," I said. "I'm plenty romantic. I'm just tuckered out."

Sassy sat down at the end of the sofa. "You need you a man who can take care of you. Some big old hunk who'll juice you right up."

"I'm not sure I want to be juicy," I complained. "Being juicy was a heap of work, and I wasn't very good at it." It was true. I'd always been tall and giraffe like. Now that I kept my white hair short and wore unisex glasses, people often said to me, "Excuse me, sir," when they bumped into me at the Walmart. It'd take a lot of work to gloss me up. At my age, I could drop dead from that much effort.

Veenie kicked off her clogs. "Bootsie thinks you're juicy. You wouldn't have to gussy anything for him."

Sassy volunteered to help glamorize me.

I flashed back to high school when Sassy had bought some Ms. Clairol blonde bomb and rubbed it into my hair. She put up my hair in orange juice can rollers and tried to convince me I looked like Marilyn Monroe. Not everyone at the Spring Fling Corn Husker's Ball had thought I looked glamorous. My cousin Harvey, aka "Snake Hips" Jones, for one, had called me Miss Andy Warhol all night long.

Sassy had moved on to her shoes and was trying to decide which pair would be best for the VFW gala. She flipped open four boxes. She held one shoe out on the flat of her hand, like Cinderella. "I can't decide which Melvin might like best. He has classic refined tastes, being a Southern gentleman and all."

Veenie choose a pair of white satin slippers with little rhinestone hearts across the stitching. "You're feet are honking big. And you've got toe corns. Those there will make your feet look more dateable."

I had to agree.

Sassy swooped back to her room to get ready for Melvin.

No sooner had Sassy disappeared than the doorbell rang. Veenie answered the door bell. It was Melvin. He was early and all gussied up. He had on a gray turtle neck and a nice white dinner jacket with white pants and patent leather shoes. He had the cutest little red carnation in his jacket button hole. He leaned on his cane a little as he came in. It was black with a fancy gold bulldog's head as the grip. "Good evening, ladies," he said.

"Howdy," I said. "Have a seat. Sassy is still getting pretty."

He sat next to Veenie in the empty recliner. "You gals not going to the dance?"

Veenie said Dickie loved to dance, but Dickie was busy working on the Chevy, trying to get the new radiator installed and the car ready for an inspection.

I said I was too pooped to tap and twirl.

"How's the ghost hunting?" he asked Veenie. "Heard you all found interesting things out at the mansion."

Veenie squinted her eyes. "How'd you hear that?"

"Read it on the *Hoosier Squealer.*"

"Tarnation," I said. "That Squeal Daddy has one big mouth."

Veenie agreed. "Where you reckon he gets his intelligence? You reckon he's following us around with one of those flying spy drones?"

"Nah, I think he gets his stories the old fashioned way. No shortage of gossips in Knobby Waters. Probably paying our neighbors to spill the beans." I meant old Mrs. Nierman. We'd both seen her with night binoculars trying to hide behind the lace curtains in her parlor while tracking our every move. Every now and then Veenie mooned her just to give her something to get all whipped up about.

Melvin asked if we'd found anything of real interest.

"Nah," I said. "Just some lights and shovels. Looks like someone has been digging late at night around the back apple trees."

"Ghosts?"

"Nah. I think we got live people involved in this."

"What on earth are they digging for?"

"Got me," I said.

"It's the treasure," said Veenie.

Melvin sat up. His ears perked up. "Treasure? Do tell."

"Alta, or her ghost, done told us she'd hid a treasure. Jedidiah's gold. The gold he stole from the town and the bank."

I felt compelled to point out to Veenie that we had no evidence at all of any treasure or gold. For all we knew, someone was digging for night crawlers.

Veenie shook her head. "Nah. Even Randy Ollis done told us there's gold out there."

Melvin asked about Randy.

Veenie explained how he was Alta's great-great-nephew, and how the Ollis family had a notion that Jedidiah had buried the gold before he fled town.

"My," said Melvin. "You two going to dig for the treasure?"

I said "No," the same time Veenie said, "Darn tootin', we are."

Sassy twirled into the room.

Melvin "ooed" and "aaahed" and helped drape a delicate crocheted shawl over Sassy's shoulders.

Sassy told us not to wait up for her.

Veenie said, "Why would we do that?"

Melvin gave us a polite, little bow goodbye. "You ladies stay out of trouble now."

As soon as Sassy was gone, I said, "I am not digging for gold."

"Who asked you to?" Veenie crunched on some Cheetos. She had an orange ring around her mouth like a clown. She washed the Cheetos down with a bottle of Big Red pop.

"You told Melvin we were going to dig for gold."

"I said 'we.' I know people other than you. Everything doesn't have to be about you, Ruby Jane."

Veenie clicked the channel over to *Bonanza* and slid up the volume. A herd of cattle thundered through the living room. We sat like that the rest of the night tossing a bag of Cheetos back and forth between us.

Chapter Twenty-One

Harry paced back and forth behind my desk. "We still got Dode on retainer?"

I'd piled a handful of bills and checks on Harry's desk earlier. I needed him to sign the checks so we could get up to date on the bills. Gratefully, Harry owned the old building and lived a cozy bachelor's life in an upstairs apartment. The downstairs we used as an office and storage. He'd inherited the building from a spinster aunt on his mom's side, so we didn't have to worry about being tossed out on our behinds.

"Darn near used up Dode's first money jar. I was waiting a piece before busting open the second one. I figure we'll need to bust it open soon to cover Kandy's second séance."

Harry stopped pacing and petted his moustache. "We got enough to cover these bills?" He picked up the stack I'd placed on his desk and rubbed the papers between his thumb and forefinger.

"Sure do." He didn't really have to ask. He knew darn well I'd not have written the checks if we couldn't make good. I'd never bounced a check in my life, and I wasn't about to start this late in the game.

"Enough to make the next payroll?"

"Nope."

We had two weeks before payroll was due again. Technically, it was Harry's job to beat the bushes, drum up business. It was his company, after all. I asked him if he had any particular new clients in mind.

He looked up from signing the bills. "Why do I always have to do every little thing around here?"

"Hold your horses there, Harry," I said. "Veenie and I found the last client. Last two clients, in fact."

That seemed to tick him off. He grabbed his hat, clutched up the paid bills, and headed toward the door. "I'll be out on the streets drumming up business to help feed you and your whackadoodle sidekick. If you need me, call. I'll be sure not to answer."

Harry bumped into Veenie as she came barreling into the office. She'd been down to the Road Kill Café loading up on day-old donuts for breakfast.

"Hey!" she cried as Harry blew past. "What's got the big boss man huffing and puffing?"

"Need some new clients. Cash is getting low again."

"Ought to advertise on the *Hoosier Squealer*. Everybody and his brother reads that rag."

"I dunno. Everybody has a heap of troubles, but nobody seems to have any cash money these days."

Veenie pulled a flier out of her pocket and smoothed it across my desk. "Here's a right nice, quick case for us. Saw this tacked on the community board at the Road Kill."

The flier read: Dog. Missing. One hundred dollar reward. Answers to the name Puddles Beesley. There was a picture of a wiener dog. He was fat and looked more like a swollen tick than a canine. The picture was fuzzy, but it looked like he was missing quite a few teeth and some whiskers too. The flier gave a number to call. Said to ask for Bet Beesley. Bet, one of Chin Wilkerson's girls, had been a year behind me in school. She'd married Pard Beesley, who was a year ahead of me in school. He was retired now, but used to drive a dump truck for the brick plant. They lived in a cute, little yellow brick bungalow right around the corner from us.

"Okeydokey," I said. "Let's go pay Bet a visit. See if she has any tips. Maybe she can tell us where Puddles likes to hang out and howl it up."

I locked up the office, and we rolled out to the go-kart, which was parked in front of the office in a spot where the meter read "expired."

"You didn't feed the meter?" I asked Veenie.

"You don't need to feed the meter if it's a go-kart."

"You sure about that?" I asked as I climbed into my orange bucket seat.

"Course I am. It's common sense. We got no license plate. I got no license. Parking laws only apply to licensed vehicles."

I had my doubts Boot would see it that way, but luckily the go-kart hadn't been ticketed.

Veenie strapped on her helmet and climbed into the driver's seat. Excited, she wiggled down into her seat and fiddled with the safety strap until she had herself tightly locked in. You would have thought we were off to the Indy 500. Veenie came alive every time we took on a new case. It didn't matter how big the case was. Her one true talent was snooping. Now that she was a paid professional snoop, nothing could dampen her spark. "I figure we can look for the pooch as we tool around town running errands. He looked mighty old in that photo, like he could pop and roll on into the Holy Hereafter anytime now."

I was about to answer when Veenie sparked up the go-kart. The thing certainly worked, maybe too well. Every time she started it up and released the hand brake, I got whip lash.

I grabbed the roll bar, and we bounced down the street in a rattling ball of exhaust smoke.

By the time we arrived at Bet's house her eyes were red as firecrackers from crying over her missing dog, Puddles. She shuffled around the kitchen in a housecoat with big pockets shaped like sunflowers on each side. Her hair was short and streaked gray. She poured us some fresh-squeezed lemonade, and we put our heads together to figure out how best to track down Puddles.

The kitchen smelled like fried chicken. Last night's supper, I reckoned. Bet handed us a photo off the refrigerator. In the photo, she was sitting on the davenport, kissing on her wiener dog. She dabbed at the corners of her eyes with a tissue as she pointed at the photo.

"Bless his little fur baby heart. He's old, but he don't know it. All his ass hair fell out couple of weeks ago. Came out in clumps. All that hair clogged up my old Hoover," Bet said as she blew her nose into a tissue. "Got the high sugar too. Needs his nightly meds."

"How'd he go missing?" I asked.

"My genius better half, Pard, left the back door open." Bet sort of yelled this in the general direction of the living room.

Pard screeched from the interior of the house, where the evening news was blaring on the TV. "I heard that, old woman!"

Bet shook her head. "He never did like that dog. Jealous of him, near as I can tell."

Pard shuffled into the kitchen, pushing a walker. "It was hot. I left the darn back door open just this one time to get me some cross breeze." He pulled a hankie out of his pocket and snorted into it. "Stupid dog must've fallen out the back door."

He's blind as a beach ball," said Bet. "Special needs dog. I got him from the wiener dog rescue."

"Well," I said, "if he's that blind, he couldn't have stumbled too far."

"You reckon?" Bet's face was lined with worry. She wiped her hands on her apron.

Veenie, who had a soft spot for dogs, told Bet not to worry. "Me and RJ have found all sorts of things. It's a senior specialty of ours."

I looked at Veenie, puzzled.

Veenie said, "Don't look at me like that. Remember when Otis Helms couldn't find his new false teeth? And we found them for him. In the refrigerator."

I looked at Bet. "They were behind the butter."

Veenie asked where Puddles liked to hang.

Bet thought for a minute. "When he was younger, he just loved to squeeze out the back gate and run down the block to party it up with Bernice, Lolly Shepherd's Saint Bernard hussy. They had a real cute litter together, back a decade ago. I mean Puddles and Bernice, not Lolly and Puddles. Anyway, they were wiener puppies with long Saint Bernard coats. Never seen anything that cute. He's tubby now. Couldn't squeeze through anything, even if he could see to make his way. He likes trash. The smell of it. Used to jump into the dumpsters down in the alley behind Pokey's. Fished him out of there once or twiced."

Pard, who'd been standing in the kitchen listening to us, loaded the wicker basket on the front of his walker with towel-wrapped, fried chicken drumsticks from the stovetop. He tossed in some napkins. He clumped back toward the living room, stopping just long enough to bend down and whisper in my ear, "I'll pay you another fifty *not* to find that smelly, little dog."

Chapter Twenty-Two

J unior slinked into the living room. He was wearing bell-bottom blue jeans and a hippie, tie-dyed T-shirt for Ben & Jerry's Wavy Gravy ice cream. His belt buckle was shaped like a giant marijuana leaf. He was wearing about a dozen strings of Mardi Gras beads. His eyes were hidden, as usual, behind round, green glasses. He slumped into the recliner next to Veenie, who was reading a Father Mackie book. "Hey, you guys know how my hog got back here?"

Without looking up from her book Veenie shook her head.

I shrugged.

Junior said, "That's funny. Cause Squeal Daddy says you do." He flicked open his iPad and held it out toward his mother. "Squeal Daddy says you were popping wheelies out by the covered bridge. He wrote you up in his police blotter section. You got no license, you realize? Riding a motorbike with no license, that's against the law, just so you know."

Veenie peered at the screen. "That's a pretty good photo of me." She went back to reading her book.

"Ma!" protested Junior. "Did you steal my bike from Pokey's for a joyride, then bring it back here?"

"Course not. Why would I do that?"

"Same reason you do everything. You're freaky."

"You got your bike back. What's it matter?" Veenie still had her nose in the book.

"Ma, the guys down at Pokey's are making fun of me."

"I wouldn't worry too much what them fellows think of you. They don't think all that often."

Darnell popped into the living room. He was wearing a red paisley do-rag. His pigtails were clean and neatly braided. He had on a crackly, old, brown leather bomber jacket and a pair of denim capris. He had a guitar slung over his back. A pair of army-green Crocs topped off his breezy rock 'n' roll look.

"Yo, Grannies!" he called. He flipped his guitar around to his front side and slumped onto the couch by my feet. "Heard you been back at that mansion snooping it up. See any more ghosts?"

"Nah," I said as I worked on my crossword puzzle. "Just found some stuff stashed outside the house."

"Like?"

"Couple of flashlights. A shovel."

"Whoa. What's that about?" Darnell had a bottle of PBR and was taking fast little slugs of it.

"Dunno," I said.

Veenie looked up from her iPad. "She knows. Someone's been poking around looking for Jedidiah's buried gold."

"For real? You mean that stolen bank gold what Randy was yacking about?"

"Randy tell you anything about that gold after that séance or while you two been knocking back drinks down at Pokey's?" Veenie asked.

"Heck no. I mean, he did mention how cool it would be if there was gold and all. How if there was gold, he reckoned he and his kin deserved some, being as how they were the rightful heirs and all."

I shook my head. "Even if there were gold—and that's a honking big IF—if it was stolen it'd belong to the town, or the people he stole it from, I reckon."

"The way Randy sees it, it's probably mostly the dowry his great-great-grandpop laid out, so Jedidiah would take Alta Iona off their hands. That being the case, wouldn't it belong to the Ollis family?"

Veenie put her book down. "Way I see it, any gold ought to belong to whoever finds it. Finders keepers."

"Oh for Pete's sake," I said. "Listen to you all talking about something that don't even exist."

"Could exist," said Veenie. "If you weren't too lazy to haul ass on out there. Dig a little."

"I'm not lazy," I defended myself. "You want us to hunt for something you made up in your head. Find me proof there's gold, and I'll start shoveling to beat the band."

That shut Veenie up.

I looked at the boys. "You two going out? Kind of late isn't it?"

Darnell finished his beer in one swallow. "We got a late-night gig over in Ewing at the Stumble On Inn. Now that Junior has his wheels back, we can rock it out of town."

Junior pumped the air with his fist. "They got speakers and mics and all. We just got to roll on in and pluck some string."

"Say, Veenie," said Darnell, as he got up from the couch. "You got an eye for fashion. These capris make my booty look appetizing? I mean, for the ladies?" He looked around, trying to get an eyeful of his own ass.

"You got a lot of ass. Like a goose. But some girls like that."

"They do?"

"Sure. You got to go with what the good Lord gave you. Play up your strengths. That's what I do."

"Thanks," said Darnell. "Later, Grannies."

And the boys were gone.

My cell phone had been vibrating. I flicked it on and scrolled through my messages. There was one from Kandy. She said the spirits were calling her. She was all juiced up for a second séance tomorrow night. We should pick her up at the

Moon Glo around seven. The other message was from Boots. It said for me to call him. "Pronto."

I told Veenie about Kandy and Boots. "What do you reckon Boots wants?" I asked.

"Didn't say anything about me, did he?" Veenie looked worried.

"You worried he saw your Evel Knievel impersonation on the *Squealer*'s website?"

"Technically, I reckon I did break the law."

"Technically???"

"The way I see it, it's ok to break a law if you're doing it for the right reasons."

"Pretty sure Boots would disagree with you on that."

"Bootsie is a stick-in-the-mud. Always was. Why you always sticking up for him?"

"I do not always stick up for him, but you know as well as I do that you do not have a legal driving license, Lavinia. Some days you can't see no better than Puddles the blind wiener dog."

"Yack. Yack. Yack. I see fine. Things are fuzzy in the middle, but you don't need to see the middle of things, just the edges. I saw it on the *Discovery* channel. You just need to see some hints, the outline. Your brain makes up the rest of it."

"Well, yours certainly does."

Chapter Twenty-Three

The next morning, Veenie and I puttered around in the go-kart. We got our weekly groceries at the Hoosier Feedbag. There was an amazing deal on pickled pig's feet, which Veenie's dad, Pappy Tuttle, loved to gnaw on. We returned Veenie's slutty library books and paid the water bill. We stopped in at the office to let Harry know we were working on a missing dog case.

But Harry was not around. I imagined he was out at the Moon Glo swapping spit with Kandy, so we left a note on his desk in case he came looking for us. Harry could get mighty touchy if he thought Veenie and I weren't putting in our forty hours of senior slave labor.

While I was scribbling the note to the boss, Veenie burst into the office, helmet askew on her head, chin strap dangling. "Move it, Ruby Jane! Think I saw Puddles!"

Outside on the sidewalk, Veenie pointed down past the Road Kill Café. I saw something brown, fat, and furry waddling down the sidewalk. It ran into the brick wall of the café and bounced back onto the sidewalk. It waddled a few more feet and slammed into the stem of a parking meter. It bounced back and slid to the left down the alley behind Pokey's place. It could have been a half-witted possum. Or a blind wiener dog.

Hoping to get a hundred bucks out of it, Veenie and I loped toward Pokey's in hot pursuit of the bouncing fur ball.

Two of the Johnson girls, Pooter's older sisters, were sitting on the limestone steps in front of Pokey's. They were wearing daisy dukes and tube tops and smoking cigarettes. They sucked on bottled Cokes. Their eyeliner was so thick it looked like they were auditioning for some kind of musical—*Rocky Horror*, maybe. They were barefooted, leaning back on the warm limestone steps, soaking up the morning sun. Toe rings glinted on their bare feet.

I asked them if they saw a dog go down the alley.

They looked at each other like I was talking foreign.

Veenie stepped up. "You two got earwax, or what?"

One of them finally spoke. "We didn't see no dog."

"Really?" said Veenie. "Like thirty seconds ago, a fat, mangy, little wiener dog didn't waddle right past you?"

The girl's mouths dropped open. "That was a dog?"

"Oh for Pete's sake," I mumbled.

Veenie and I took off around the corner of the alley.

There were three dumpsters in the alley. Each was overflowing. A stack of used pallets and pizza boxes towered on each side of the dumpsters. The whole mess smelled like oil, grease, rotten food, cigarettes, and beer, with a sprinkle of urine. It was a warm day, and the trash was in the sunlight. The rubber bottom of my right canvas tennis shoe stuck to the pavement as we tried to creep toward the dumpsters.

Veenie got excited when she saw a tail wagging between two bag wrappers marked "mystery meat" and a stack of rotten cabbages.

"Here poochie! Here poochie! That you Puddles? Come to Auntie Veenie, Puddles."

The tail stopped wagging. Whatever it was, its head and front paws were stuck in a mystery meat bag. Maybe it heard Veenie. Maybe it was stuck on something inside the bag. Maybe it was busy suffocating itself. Hey, growing old ain't for everybody.

Veenie said maybe we should just creep up on the ass end of the thing and grab hold of the tail as tightly as we could.

I tried to slide forward, but I was sticking to the pavement. My right foot was stuck to a wad of what looked to be melting pink bubble gum and a condom. "I'm stuck tight," I said.

"Oh Lord," Veenie complained. "It's always something with you."

"You go on. I'll work on scraping my foot loose." I leaned against the brick tavern wall and looked around for something to scrape my shoe on. I saw a crushed Bud Light can, cut almost in two, and plucked it out of the pile of trash. I did a one-legged flamingo stand and went at my shoe, trying to get the gum off without falling over and busting every other part of me.

Veenie was half-gone into the trash pile now. The tail had disappeared into a dumpster. She was climbing up a rickety stack of pallets, giving chase. I was starting to have a bad feeling.

The tail disappeared. Then something ran out past me so fast I almost did the splits. Whatever it was, it had a few whiskers and milky eyes. Butt mange too.

Veenie came crashing down with the pile of pizza boxes. Luckily, she landed ass first on a rotten bag of produce. "You catch Puddles?"

I had the gum off my shoe now. "No, but I think he's got himself trapped," I said.

The little dog was bouncing back and forth between bags of trash. A puddle of what looked to be beer caught his nose. He stood there, paw-deep in the puddle. He started lapping to beat the band. He stopped only to belch and fart.

I took a couple of steps closer to Puddles. Got down on my knees to see what the little fellow was doing. "That dog is drunk."

"Course he is. No accident we found him rolling in the gutter here out behind Pokey's."

By this time, he'd lapped up the giant puddle of beer.

"He likes beer?"

"Who doesn't? You ask me, that dog is an alkie. Only person I ever saw suck up a puddle of beer that fast was my ex, Fergus Senior."

I supposed dogs could be addicts. I'd read once that elephants could get drunk on rotten jungle fruits. Then once, at a class at the ag extension, one of them college professors they carted in from Purdue to teach scientific farming techniques to hillbillies told us that the first thing mankind ever wrote down over there in Egypt, cradle of civilization, was a beer recipe. That sounded about right to me. For my part, I wasn't about to tell Bet Beesley that her precious fur baby was a boozehound.

"He okay?" I asked.

"He looks awful, but I think that's his natural look."

I hunkered down and inspected Puddles. He was missing some whiskers. And a lot of teeth. While I was inspecting him, he fell over on one side. He lay there on the pavement panting like a furry Bratwurst. I propped him up. He coughed and farted at the very same time. I backed up. My toes felt warm. And wet. I looked down to see a puddle of yellow. I could see now where the dog had gotten his name. I was beginning to see a couple of reasons why Pard had been so eager to let Puddles do a free Willy.

Veenie scooped up Puddles and we ambled toward the go-kart, anxious to claim our hundred bucks.

Bet screamed with delight when Veenie handed Puddles over to her in the kitchen. He was tinkling a stream even as the hand-off occurred, but Bet didn't seem to mind it. She yelled for Pard to come mop up the dribble off the linoleum.

Bet was smooching Puddles to death when she suddenly stopped. She did a double sniff of the dog's breath. She held him out at arm's length and studied him. "Lord. Is he drunk?" She looked at Veenie, and her eyes narrowed in suspicion.

"Found him like that," said Veenie. "In the alley behind Pokey's."

"What kind of lowlife would get a little doggie drunk?"

"I think he ran away to get at some beer. Maybe you better send him to that Triple A."

Bet looked puzzled. "You mean AA?"

"Whatever works for liquored-up dogs."

Bet kissed Puddles on the forehead again. She hugged him so hard he tinkled on her again. She wiped at it with a wet paper towel.

"His bladder is getting weak," she said. "Vet said it's the high sugar. Lord, I sure do appreciate your finding him for me. I was afraid he was a goner."

Bet crossed the kitchen and pulled our fee out of the cookie jar. The jar was shaped like a giant strawberry with a fat bumble bee as the top stopper. She counted out the money patiently, one bill at a time. There were a lot of crumpled ones.

Veenie flattened the pile of bills, rolled them around her finger, and then stuck them into her bra. "Much obliged. Call us anytime you lose anything of value. That includes Pard. We offer senior specials."

We said our good-byes and scooted out the back door.

I saw Pard glowering at us out from behind the lace curtains in the kitchen as we lurched away in the go-kart. I'm pretty sure he was shooting us the double bird.

Chapter Twenty-Four

The Impala was still at the Lube It Up shop getting new guts, so Harry agreed to drive us out to Dode's farm for the séance. Unlike before, the weather was bright and clear. Just enough heat that you didn't quite need a jacket.

Harry pulled up to our house and laid on the horn. Kandy was in the front seat snuggled so close she could have been a tick stuck to Harry's side. She was wearing his hat and smoking one of his cigarettes when we came out of the house.

Kandy threw me and Veenie a handy hello as we climbed into the back of the Toyota.

"Evening gals. You ready to chat up the dead?" She blew smoke out the window, which was rolled down and letting in a nice breeze.

Veenie leaned up and asked Kandy if she was sure she could conjure a spirit, the weather being so nice and mild.

"Oh sure." She untangled from Harry, returned his hat to his head, and turned to face us in the back seat. Her hair was twisted up in a bun with long curls falling like sideburns close to her ears. She was wearing an off-the-shoulder peasant blouse and double silver-loop earrings. Her eye shadow was thick and sky blue, like her eyes. "Alta Iona done came to me in a dream. Promised she'd make an appearance."

I said, "Thought you didn't offer guarantees."

"I don't, sugar. But when the spirits right out say they'll do something, they do it, all righty."

Veenie seemed impressed. "Wish living people were so conscientious."

"Me too," said Kandy. "Specially men. I swear they think with their willies."

"Nah," said Veenie. "Most of them don't think at all."

Harry coughed an objection.

I asked Harry if he got the hundred bucks we left on his desk.

"Yeah. That for the dog?" He said as he headed up the winding knobs toward Dode's farm.

Kandy asked if we'd bought a dog. "Just love them little purse dogs. I'd have me one, but I travel too much."

"Nah," Veenie said. "We found Bet Beesley's dog. Blind wiener dog. He ran away. Found him down at Pokey's, tying one on. Collected the reward money for Harry."

Harry glanced at us in the rearview. "You realize how silly that sounds, right?"

"Silly or not, that's what happened, right RJ?"

"Yep."

Kandy seemed intrigued. "The Shades Agency finds missing pets?" She addressed her remark to Harry.

Harry twisted his lips. He grunted. "Hell no. I mean, not really. Those two like to help out their senior pals, so I humor them."

Veenie poked her head up. "Harry's just embarrassed. He thinks he's Magnum, PI. Too proud to be seen rounding up drunk dogs. Makes us old ladies do all the work."

"Not true," protested Harry. "Stop telling people that. You'll have social services on me for elder abuse. People take shit like that serious these days."

"Yeah," Veenie said. "Not like the good old days when you could pistol-whip grandma and leave her to rot in the cellar like a sack of taters."

"Oh for Pete's sake," said Harry. "No one has ever pistol-whipped you, Lavinia. I've seen you knocking people in the head with the butt of that BB gun."

"I'm old. I got to protect myself. My bones are like Jell-O. Thinking of getting me one of those stun guns."

"No," said Harry. "Absolutely not."

"Who asked you?"

Thankfully, we pulled into Dode's yard, and they both shut up. In fact, we were all a little speechless. We weren't the only ones parked in Dode's yard. The Pawpaw County Sheriff's car was backed in, front end out, tucked close to the porch. Dode was sitting on the porch in his customary rocker. Devon Hattabaugh, the junior law officer, was sitting next to him.

"Uh-oh," said Veenie.

"Oh shit," said Harry.

Kandy just slid out of the car, trounced up to the porch, and started introducing herself to Devon.

By the time we all got on the porch, Kandy was sitting next to Devon, reading his palm. Devon wore his beret. His muttonchop whiskers had been shaved down close to his face. His aviator sunglasses were clipped to the V pocket of his shirt. He seemed enchanted.

Kandy explained to Devon that he had a generous heart and would have many lovers. She stroked a couple spots on his palm then flashed some Chiclet teeth at him.

Devon nodded. "I always thought so. I mean, about the heart. I went into law enforcement because there was a major for that at the community college, and my mama was in favor of having an officer in the family. But if I'd had my druthers I would have studied philosophy. I like to think about things. I'm kind of deep inside."

"I bet you write poetry."

"How'd you know that?"

Kandy traced a place under Devon's ring finger. "See that itty-bitty line?"

"Uh-huh."

"That tells me you are an artist. And lookie here, that says you're going to be famous."

Devon beamed. "I was mentioned twice in the *Hoosier Squealer* this month. Got my picture in the sheriff's association newsletter too. Recruit of the month in Pawpaw County."

Veenie leaned over and whispered to me, "Weren't he the only recruit?"

"Still counts."

Kandy laid it on thicker. She slapped it on with a cement trowel. "This here line is all about you being a hero. Some men got no line here at all." She glanced up at Harry. "But you got a double-chained line."

"That good?"

"Heck yeah. The best. A double chain is like hero stuff."

Devon's eyes were bright as stars now. "Like Batman?"

"Yeah. Something like that." Kandy let go of Devon's hand and shook out her hair. She adjusted her hoop ear rings. She asked Devon if he was coming to the séance.

He squirmed a little.

I told him he was sure enough invited. "Last time we saw a ghost."

He looked me dead in the eye. "There's no such thing as ghosts."

Kandy objected. "Why, Devon, there is so such a thing as ghosts. And we all seen this one, didn't we?" She looked at Dode, who was bobbing his head so fast it looked like it might roll off.

Devon stood up and stretched his legs. He walked around the porch, his hands clutched to his gun belt. "Can't let you have that séance. Sheriff Gibson sent me out here personally to make sure there's no more trespassing. That mansion and all that land is part of a crime scene. You can't be messing with that."

Kandy stood up next to Devon and put her hands on his shoulders. In heels, she was a bit taller than him. In terms of manipulating men, she was a giant next to him.

His shoulders fell and relaxed a bit.

"Sugar, we got to let that ghost talk. She can't get no peace until she tells us who killed her. What if this was your mama? You wouldn't want to keep an innocent soul from getting on to heaven, would you?"

Devon looked uncertain. "Hang it," he said. "It ain't me. This is my job. I swore to uphold the law. If I don't uphold the law, Sheriff Gibson is bound to get mad. And he's ugly and mighty mean when he's mad."

I stepped forward. "You want to solve this crime, right?"

He nodded.

"Us too. Why not think of this ghost as a witness? If you went with us and you talked to her, you'd be interrogating the chief witness. Ain't that doing your job too?"

"Well ... I reckon it might be."

Harry threw his two cents into the ring. "Look, son, we don't want you to get into trouble, but Kandy is right. This is a matter of a woman's soul. She's got to unburden her soul or else she'll never get to pass on to heaven. I mean, do you want to risk being the person who answers to that on that other side? I sure wouldn't want to risk that kind of damnation."

"Damnation???" That got Devon's attention. "I dunno. I never heard of anything like this in Sunday school."

Veenie asked what church he was raised in.

"Methodist," he said. "My mama's people were Methodists."

Veenie said, "I been to all the churches, and I can tell you this here could be a mortal sin in every single one of them, except maybe the Holy Rollers. Heck, when they start yacking in tongues, no one knows what they're talking about. Most of them don't know either."

Devon was close to breaking down. We were all older than him. And we had him confused. That meant we had the advantage.

I could tell he was about to give in and let us have the séance when a pickup truck, lights flashing, slid into the yard and parked tight to the porch. Boots got out of the driver's side. It was his truck, with one of those portable roof cherries slapped on top. He used his truck like this when on official business if Devon had the squad car.

And Boots wasn't alone. The passenger side door popped open. Melvin Beal slid out. His white hair was all neat, plastered to his head. He wasn't dressed in a turtleneck and patent leather loafers, like a southern mama's boy, though. He was wearing a black windbreaker, white button-down shirt, and black creased trousers. The words "US Treasury, Enforcement," were stitched across his jacket.

"Uh-oh," said Veenie. "It's the Feds."

Chapter Twenty-Five

We ended up in jail.

"You can't keep us here!" cried Veenie. "I'm old. I got those Miranda rights, the constitutional right not to get myself into trouble. I got a bad heart. I feel like I might fall over. I might die." She clutched at her heart and twirled around in circles. When that didn't get her any response she fell backward onto a cot and panted like Puddles.

No one paid her any mind.

We were huddled together on some iron benches in the holding cell in the Pawpaw County jail. Me, Veenie, Kandy, Harry, and Dode. The cell did double-duty as the local drunk tank. That night we were in there with Chigger Shelton. He'd tied one on at Pokey's, and Pokey had carried him over for a sleepover. He was a tiny, dark-skinned guy, no bigger 'round than a bobby pin. He was so nearsighted his red, plastic glasses, which were held together with silver duct tape, made his brown eyes bug out. He was rolled up in a gray blanket like a roly-poly bug. Every now and then he'd sit up and mumble. He'd take wild swats at something around his ears and the back of his head. Then he'd roll up like a bug again.

Veenie wanted to tell him about the ghosts and how he she was being manhandled by the law, but he wasn't having any part of it. He stuck his fingers in his ears.

Melvin approached the cell, carrying a ring of keys. "Sorry to lock all you folks up like this, but we need to determine what you all know, and this was the best way I could think of for getting you all to calm down and talk to us."

He took me and Veenie first and led us into the back room where they kept the cleaning supplies, then over to the break room. When Veenie whined about having a dry throat and maybe fainting, he gave us paper cups of cold water from the cooler. He motioned to the break table and rolled a mop bucket out of the way so we could all squeeze in around the table.

"Now, ladies, tell me what you know." He had a pen and pad poised on his knee.

"Nothing," I said. "Like, I don't even know why you brought us here. I thought you sold liquor for a living."

"Did. Used to work with alcohol and firearms. I'm with the Treasury Department now. We do asset recovery. I was sent here by the Louisville Office of Recovery. We believe that you and Mrs. Goens may have some very valuable assets that belong to the United States Government. My job is to recover those assets."

Veenie popped up in her chair. "It's the gold, ain't it? Jedidiah buried gold out at that mansion, didn't he? Tarnation, I knew there was a treasure. I just knew it."

Melvin blinked, but his face stayed blank. "Is there a treasure?"

I eyed Melvin. "Don't you know?"

"We know that you and Mrs. Goens have been fencing stolen federal property around town."

Veenie's face fell. "We have?"

I asked Veenie what she knew about these allegations.

She shrugged. "I swear on my mama's grave, the only stolen loot I've touched is Junior's Harley. And that was just to get the thing back from whoever snatched it to begin with. You mean Junior's bike? I mean, he bought that bike fair and square off Sammy Spray over in Salem. It's got papers and all. If it belongs to the government, I'll smack Junior for being stupid enough to buy it and he'll apologize and give it back."

Melvin scraped back his chair and stood. "Look, ladies, if you come clean, there might be a finder's fee. I might be able to get a deal for you."

I was starting to feel like we were in some deep doo-doo. The Feds. Felony possession of US Government property. And there I sat, as clueless as Puddles bouncing off brick walls. I was pretty sure this was not about Junior's stolen Harley or the murder of Alta Iona a hundred years ago.

"Could you help us out? Tell us exactly what stolen property we've been passing around town?"

Melvin reached over and shook out a manila envelope. A plastic bag thumped out on the table. "This, for starters."

I picked up the bag and worried it between my fingers until I could see through the plastic clearly. It was a large golden dollar coin. There were two eagles on one side. Ms. Liberty was on the other side. It was inscribed "1861" and "Confederate States of America."

"We've never seen that," I said. I pushed it back toward Melvin.

Veenie stood on tiptoe, yanked off her glasses, and bent down to inspect the coin. "Uh-oh."

"Veenie?" I said.

"I might have seen that before. Once. Maybe. Not saying I did. Not saying I didn't." She looked a little panicked.

She swerved her head to face Melvin. "I don't see too well. You can't send a blind old lady to jail."

I looked at Melvin. "Could you excuse us for a moment, please?"

Melvin plucked his cane from where it was hooked on the table edge and ambled back out into the main office and holding cell area. He shut the door gently behind him.

Veenie chewed on her little fingernail. "I seen that coin before, I think."

"Where?"

"In Dode's money jar."

"You mean the moldy money you took to the bank to cash in for Dode's retainer?"

"Uh-huh. There were a couple of funny coins in there. But the coin counter in the bank lobby took them okay. That one he showed us I kind of remember because it said it's a Confederate coin, and well, they lost the war, so I figured it was a joke. A dummy coin. I put it in the counter hoping to mooch an extra dollar off that old tightwad, Avonelle Apple. She must have called the Feds. Turned us in. She never did have much of a sense of humor."

I inspected the coin. In the bottom left, where the mint mark showed on modern coins, there was a "D - Dahlonega, Georgia" strike mark. To my knowledge there was no "Dahlonega" mint in the United States. No mint in Georgia ever, that I knew of.

"1861 would have been near the end of the Civil War. Veenie, I think that coin is for real."

I fired up the Internet browser on my cell phone and searched for keywords related to the coin's date and description. "Holy Jesus!" I said. "Lord Almighty!"

"What?" Veenie was on her toes, straining to see over my shoulder.

"That is a Confederate Double Eagle coin. One of an uncirculated batch that was minted by the Confederate government just as the war was near over. Only coins ever minted in Georgia. A shipment of them were robbed off a train in rural Georgia after being confiscated by the Union Army and routed north to the Union Treasury for a meltdown."

"You mean it's real?"

"Real and worth …" I couldn't say that big a number out loud. It stuck to the roof of my mouth. I pointed to the estimated valuation on the phone screen. That coin was worth a quarter of a million dollars.

Veenie screamed and dropped the coin bag. The coin spilled out and rolled under the pop machine. "Oh shit!" said Veenie. She danced around like she had to go to the bathroom. She dropped to her knees, mashed the side of her head to the cement floor, and tried to see under the pop machine.

"Can't see it," she said. She tried, unsuccessfully, to slip her fat fingers under the pop machine. She drew her hand back and stared at her dirty, sticky fingernails.

"Veenie?"

"Yeah?"

"Were there more of those coins?"

"I dunno. I didn't look at every single coin, Ruby Jane. Cleaned them a little. Dumped them into the wide, metal mouth of that coin machine in the lobby. I remember that one because it got stuck. And it was all pinky-gold in color. I remember thinking what a hoot it would be to see Avonelle's face when she saw we'd given her a slug coin from a country that don't even exist."

"Where you think Dode got that coin?"

"Jeepers. Dode must have found the treasure. Out on his farm. Threw it in with his emergency coin bank for safekeeping."

The door creaked open. Melvin came back in. Kandy was with him. She waved our way. Her gypsy bracelets clattered like castanets.

"Got to tinkle," she said. "Won't take me but a minute. Go right ahead with your talking gals. I'll turn on the water, so you don't hear me making my business."

Melvin showed her to the bathroom. It was back behind the break room wall and pop machine. He stood there in the hallway, his hands behind his back, waiting for her to finish her business. He had taken off his jacket and was wearing a shoulder holster.

I told Melvin how we came to have the one coin. I explained to him our theory that Dode must have found that piece of lost gold and that we got it innocently by accident when he gave us his money jars.

"How much was there in that batch of stolen Confederate coins?" I asked.

Melvin checked his pocket watch. He shook his head at how long Kandy was taking. "One hundred coins, never circulated. Only forty ever showed up. Down in Mexico, a couple of months after Jedidiah left town. Back then, the Treasury agents tracked Jedidiah as far as Mexico City. It was him and his men who robbed that train in Georgia. He came up to Knobby Waters under a new name and used some of the gold melted down to set himself up to look like a big shot. When the agents finally found him, he used the flood as an excuse to run again. Because of the flood, we don't think he could get back to where he had hidden most of the gold."

"The rest of the original Confederate gold is missing?

"Missing since the train robbery. Never circulated. I'm with cold cases. We wait for coins like this to show up. Track down the owners. Some people steal these kinds of coins, keep them hidden for decades. Once they show up in the money stream, we hunt down the origin. Trace them back to the original thief. Like in this case."

Melvin put his ear to the bathroom door. His face collapsed into a frown. He knocked at the door. No answer.

"Oh, dang it!" He backed up and kicked at the door with his tasseled loafers. It swung open. The bathroom was empty. The window was wide open, and there was no sign of Kandy.

"Gosh darn!" he said. "Can't believe she gave me the slip."

Veenie stared at the empty bathroom. "Why'd she run?"

154

Boots Gibson strolled into the break room and answered that question. "She's a con artist. Wanted in six states for fraud. Travels around swindling old folks by putting on ghost séances."

Boots had a tiny handheld projector smaller than a cell phone and some files under his arm. He sat them down on the table. He showed us some black and white photos. "This look like your ghost?"

Veenie nodded. "Yep, that's Alta."

"Ain't Alta," said Boots. "It's just some generic ghost film she projects onto walls out of the tiny hole in this pocket projector. Found it on her when we booked her into the cell. One set of images is male. One is female. She pulled the same con two weeks ago over in a small town outside St. Louis. Got this old lady believing her husband was back as a spirit telling her to donate all her money to some church. Kandy was the minister of that church, of course."

I stared at Boots.

He stared back.

He whispered into my ear. "You ought to return my calls, woman," he said. "I might just know a thing or two."

"I'm all ears. What else do you know?"

"Plenty."

"Like."

"I'll tell you over dinner tomorrow night."

"I'm not going on any date. Not at my age."

"It's not a date. It's a fish fry. I caught most of the fish. Least you could do is come eat some of it. Seven o'clock. Boat and Gun Club."

Chapter Twenty-Six

"This is blackmail," I said. "Extortion. Sexual exploitation."

"This here is a free dinner," said Boots. "Shut your yapper. Eat up, Ruby Jane."

We were at the White River Boat and Gun Club. It was the annual Boy Scout fish fry, about as romantic as it got for weekend dates in Pawpaw County, unless you got invited to the Steinkamp's fall Pig Poke, Beer Garden, and Sauerkraut Extravaganza, or Ma and Peepaw Horton's annual Chicken-landia BBQ chicken benefit for the old folks out at Leisure Hills.

I wasn't complaining, at least not about the food.

Pard Beesley was wearing his triangular Boy Scout troop leader hat and bibbed BBQ apron. He was hand-dipping catfish fillets in a beer cornmeal batter and expertly tossing them into an oil barrel fry pit. The fire leapt and the pot sizzled. He had his walker fitted with a row of canvas pockets and hooks. He had different spatulas and seasoning jars dangling in close reach off the contraption. The air smelled like sweet fried fish and hush puppies. The air was damp enough for a sweater. Crickets chirped above the sizzle of the fryer.

Puddles the wiener dog was under Pard's walker, catching hush puppy bits that fell his way. After a while, he was so tired of snapping at the air that he fell over. He was snoring in the sand under the fryer pit when Bet found him. She scooped him up and tucked him into the cloth baby carrier she had strapped to her chest.

"Have some taters," said Boots. He spooned heaps of crisp tater tots and onions onto my paper plate and tossed on a couple of fat slabs of corn bread with butter pats.

I did not resist.

He grabbed a pair of Budweiser beers out of the ice tub and popped the tops while holding both cans in one of his big, hammy, red hands. He offered me one fizzing can.

We scooched onto a seat at a picnic table on the screened-in porch next to Harry. Harry was sitting alone, with his hat pulled over his eyes, sulking. Melvin and the Feds had confiscated Dode's money jars. We no longer had any retainer. We were out a few hundred dollars with no new cases in sight, and Kandy had left him high and dry, taking his home stereo system, TV, microwave, and laptop computer. She'd also cleaned out his liquor cabinet, the good stuff anyway. He was left with little more than his moustache and a bottle of Mad Dog to suck on.

"Cheer up," I said to Harry. "Not like Kandy was the love of your life."

"Maybe not, but she was good company." He sniffled a little then chewed on the crisp tip of a battered fish. "We're dead broke, you know."

"Yeah, well, we've been there before. Something will turn up."

"What?" Harry moaned, "A missing herd of cats?"

Boots polished off his first fish sandwich and shoveled back a couple of spoonful's of tater tots smothered in ketchup and fried onions. "You all could go for the bail bounty."

"On Kandy?"

"Gosh, no. On Darnell." Boots attacked a second sandwich, this one piled high with cold slaw and mustard.

My mouth fell open. "You want to tell us more about that?"

"Oh sure," he mumbled as he poked some loose cold slaw into the corner of his mouth. "I tried to tell you all this, but you never returned my calls."

I felt the heat rise in my cheeks. "Darn it, Boots. I'm talking to you now. What's the deal with Darnell?"

"He's the one who's been living in that Gremlin. Stole it over in Washington County."

"No kidding."

"It's a crime, Ruby Jane. I don't kid about that. And just for the record, he's the one who stole Junior's Harley. Got a long record. Everything he touches sticks to him like toffee."

Harry was sitting up now, fiddling with the rim of his hat. "What's his bounty?"

"Couple of thousand, if you bring him in over in Washington County."

"You'd let that happen?" I asked.

"I'm not on quota here, Ruby Jane. Makes no difference to me who brings him in, but you'd have to find him."

"How you know he stole that Gremlin and Junior's hog?"

"Pooter. I picked him up and shook the spit out of him until he squealed. Don't know if Darnell is still in county. The Feds busting your séance probably spooked him."

"Why would he care about the séance and the Feds? He didn't commit a federal crime."

"Not so sure about that."

"Give," I said.

Boots drained his beer and went to get another one. When he got back he told me that April, the coroner, had called him right before he picked me up for dinner. "She got the results back from that skeleton and ran the DNA through the federal crime database. Turns out that skeleton, Alta Iona Ollis, matches a couple of Ollis guys doing time over in Missouri for murder and larceny."

"Not Randy Ollis?"

"Nah. The skeletal DNA would probably match him, yeah, but he's never been arrested. We don't have him in the crime database. She did match someone else we know, though."

"Who?"

"Your sticky-fingered houseguest, Darnell Zikes."

"Darnell?"

"Yep. He's Alta Iona's great-great-grandson. No doubt about it."

I let that piece of news sink in. "So, it's no accident that he showed up here and was hanging with me and Veenie asking about the mansion and all."

"I'm thinking not. Thinking he saw the news on the *Squealer*'s website and moseyed over this way to see if he could get his hands on some kind of inheritance."

"Why would he do that?"

Boots shrugged. "Want some cake? They got a carrot sheet cake. Bet Beesley made it. I'm having a hunk or two."

"Sure," I said.

While Boots was off getting us cake, Veenie strolled over to our table. She was drinking a Big Red pop out of the bottle with two straws. She was wearing a sleeveless, lime-green tunic and a really wide pair of polka dot culottes. She had on white, patent leather go-go boots with purple tassels that she got off the Widow Guthrie at the Lutheran community yard sale. The Widow's oldest daughter, Ramona, had been a majorette for the Corn Huskers marching band, back in the seventies.

"On a date, I see," she said.

"No," I said. "N-O. This is a business dinner. Boots is filling me in on the mansion mystery."

"Dickie has the Impala fixed up. Said he'd bring it around tomorrow."

Dickie waved at me from across the porch, where he was in line at the buffet loading two paper plates with fried fish and taters.

I waved back. "That Dickie's a keeper," I said. Men our age knew how to fix stuff. Get things done. Men these days, not so much.

My cell started jumping. It was Dode, so I answered.

"Them ghosts are back!"

"There are no ghosts, Dode. We told you, Kandy made all that up. She was trying to scare you. Get money out of you."

"Nope. I got ghosts. I know what I'm looking at, missy."

"Are they out under the apple trees again?"

"Yep. Like before. Got their big butt lights on."

"You want us to come on over?"

"Course I do! They might give me the slip. I aim to catch them red-handed this time. You all park down the road in the tractor pull-off. Walk on up. I'll keep an eye on them until you all get here. I got my rifle loaded, so if they try and give me the slip, I'll blow holes through them so big they'll think hell is the friendly place."

Chapter Twenty-Seven

Dode was telling the truth, per usual.

We all parked in the tractor pull-off down from the apple orchard and circled our vehicles together like covered wagons defending against a ghost attack. With night binoculars provided by Boots, we had a clear line of sight down to the orchard. The binoculars revealed a pair of bright green blurs, shaped like fuzzy people, moving around under the trees. They looked to be digging. We couldn't tell much in the way of details.

Dode was dancing around, all excited. "Hot diggity! Now, how we going to catch them ghosts?"

Boots was studying the situation. He was swinging the binoculars back and forth, up and down, all around the mansion. "Dode, you sure were right. You got something going on over there."

Veenie snatched the binoculars. "You reckon it's someone looking for that gold? Did Melvin, that Fed agent, say anything about if they'd found all the gold?"

Boots sniffled. "He's not sure. Said there were only two coins recovered from Dode's jars. Ought to be another twenty coins somewhere."

I said they could have been lost in the flood or spent down in Mexico and just never reported.

"Could be," said Boots.

I was thinking to myself that two coins weren't so bad, given that these coins were worth half a million. Not bad for spare pocket change kept in a cellar jar all those years. I said if someone were still digging then, in their minds, there was more gold or more of something worth turning earth for. "If we got closer, reckon we could make out more about who's doing what down there?"

Boots said, "Yeah, but you ladies aren't going down there."

Veenie objected. "Bootsie, it's our case. You gave it to us. Why you want to take it back now?"

"I gave it to you when I thought it was nonsense involving dead people and ghosts. Now that it's federal and we're talking millions and it involves live people, it's in my jurisdiction."

Dode made a little sound in his throat. "Ghosts on the move! They're moving. Toward the mansion. Into the mansion."

It was dark again under the apple trees. Boots unholstered his gun. "I'm closing in. You all stay put right here. Don't move. I'll get to the bottom of this."

He looked at Veenie. "Don't you dare follow me either, Lavinia. I don't want to accidently shoot your head off. Ruby Jane there would never forgive me."

Boots moved off into the high weeds, quiet and stealth for a big guy.

Veenie eyed me. "I can't just stand here and wait." She was hopping from foot to foot, all agitated. She had her BB pistol raised in one hand. She waved the pistol. "Come on, Ruby Jane."

Veenie took my hand and we were off into the low corn on the opposite side of the mansion from the side Boots was tracking in on.

Dode whispered after us to be careful.

Veenie and I found a low window around back where the boards had been pried off. There was an old oil drum close to the window. I held the BB pistol and boosted up Veenie onto the drum. I handed her the pistol. She used it to bust the rest of the boards off the window. She straddled the window but managed to get the seat of her culottes stuck on a nail that was protruding out of the window sill. She kicked up a fuss. Her white majorette go-go boots glowed in the moonlight, making her look like she was trying to ride a stubborn mule.

"You stuck?" I whispered.

"Leg of my culottes is."

"Can you wiggle out of them?"

"Think so."

Veenie squirmed and wiggled and at last was able to slide over the window sill into the house. I heard a little thump as she hit the floor on the other side. Her culottes were hanging on a nail in the window, waving in the breeze. I had no doubt that picture would somehow end up on the Squealer's website, along with an inappropriately suggestive title about this whole case. What the heck. The only reputation I had to protect these days was a bad one.

I hoisted myself up into the window, careful to avoid the nail that had claimed Veenie's pants. I landed behind Veenie on the other side. We were in a part of the house I'd not seen before. It looked to be a back sitting parlor. I raked a spider web off my face. Veenie was standing there in a beam of moonlight. Her white majorette boots glowed. Her dimpled knees shined like scabby apples. She was wearing a solid pair of baggy granny panties and didn't seem at all upset about having lost her pants. Veenie was like that. She'd run butt naked through the fires of hell for a chance at an adventure.

"Follow me," she whispered, her BB pistol held high in both hands. Her hands were shaking a little, so the BBs were rattling, but she managed to get a tighter grip on the pistol and quiet the gun down.

My heart was thumping a good bit. It was dark as an ink well in the interior of the house, and the place smelled dank and moldy. I muffled a sneeze in my shirt tail a couple of times. Nobody home but dust and spiders. I doubted Veenie knew where we were going. I just hoped it wasn't toward Boots because he had more than BBs in his gun.

And he never had liked Veenie all that much.

We heard a creaking sound overhead. Veenie decided to follow that. We crawled very slowly up the stairs trying hard to avoid any squeaky boards, but no matter which way we moved, the house creaked and groaned. We arrived on a landing that rolled out into a long, broad hallway. Quite a few doors lined the hallway. It was quiet. No sign of any living thing.

An idea popped in my head. I slid my cell out of my pocket and clicked on a flashlight app. It wasn't the brightest, but by getting down on my knees, I could spray the light along the dusty floor. I saw a long trail where the dust had been cleared, by people walking, no doubt. The trail led to the end of the hallway. That door was shut.

"I think someone went into that room at the end of the hallway," I whispered to Veenie.

"Okeydokey. Stay behind me. Tight."

We scooted that way. Once we arrived at the closed door, I wasn't sure what to do. Veenie seemed to know. She put her hand on the knob, and the door creaked open.

There was somebody in that room all righty.

Veenie stopped short in front of me and screamed like a snake had run up her leg.

"Lord Almighty!" gruffed Boots as he slid into the beams of moonlight that flooded the room. He lowered his gun. "Jesus Christ Almighty!" Don't you two old nincompoops ever listen to a word I say? I could have splattered your heads like watermelons." Boots studied Veenie, who still had her BB gun pointed at his belly. Her dimpled knees shined in the dim light, all white and scabby. Her baggy old lady panties looked a good bit like a diaper.

"Lavinia Goens," said Boots, "are you not wearing any pants? Are you, honest to God, half-naked like I think you are?"

I was about to explain about Veenie's attire and object to being called a nincompoop when I heard an engine start up outside. A car sputtered and choked to life. Not a very new car or a car in very good mechanical working order either, from the sound of it.

I tiptoed over and peered out the slit left by a broken board nailed at an angle across the upstairs hallway window. The window looked out toward the main road in front of Dode's farm.

A vehicle flashed past Dode's farmhouse. The security lights by the barn burst on. A purple Gremlin sped by and then disappeared as the barn's pole lights blinked off. The Gremlin was missing one red taillight. It disappeared around a corner in the gravel road and headed down the knobs toward town.

"Dang it! Our ghost got away," I said.

Chapter Twenty-Eight

It was late by the time we got home, and a chill was in the air. The porch lights were on, bright enough so that a swarm of insects were buzzing in the spray of light. Sassy was sitting on the porch swing. Melvin was sitting next to her. He was out of his Fed uniform now, dressed in his mama boy turtleneck and creased trousers again. He threw us a little wave and a smile.

Sassy gave us the cold shoulder.

Veenie walked up to them. "Why didn't you tell us lover boy there was a Fed?"

"Didn't know," said Sassy. "Thought he was a high-class liquor salesman, same as you." She was dressed in a pink, Angora V-neck sweater with white neck pearls. She had on white stockings and a nice, very short, navy, knit pencil skirt. Her eyebrows were painted on so high they looked like McDonald's arches.

Melvin blinked behind his thick glasses. He had one arm swung around Sassy's shoulders. "I'm a special agent. We try and enter a situation under a trustworthy identity. We get more information that way. Didn't mean you ladies no harm. Didn't expect to get Miss Sassy here out of the deal. But mighty glad I did." He gave Sassy a cheek peck.

She glowed like she'd been hit with a pair of radioactive lips.

I was curious, so I asked about the case and the gold. "Your boys still searching the mansion for gold?"

"Nope. We did a thorough search. Used ground detectors and probes. If the rest of the gold coins are in that apple orchard, they are lost forever."

"Ever heard tell of a guy named Darnell Zikes?"

"Oh, sure. Boots told me he's been hanging around. Wanted for crimes down south. He's the fellow whose DNA matched up with that skeleton, isn't he?"

"Yeah, that's him. Alta Iona and Jedidiah's great-great-grandson, it seems."

"Why you asking?"

"Pretty sure he was out at the mansion digging around tonight."

"Well, he's welcome to dig all he wants. My boss is satisfied there's nothing more out there. Property belongs to the county. Been abandoned for decades. Don't think anyone cares what happens out there now. Even if he finds more gold, it belongs to the federal government. He can't fence it. We'd be on him like flies on fresh manure."

"Thanks," I said.

Veenie trounced into the house ahead of me.

Sassy stood up a little and stared after Veenie. "Ruby Jane, I don't think Lavinia was wearing any pants. Was she honest to God not wearing any pants?" She was holding one hand to her breastplate.

"I dunno," I mumbled, not caring to get into the sordid details or have my shut-eye delayed by listening to Sassy yammer on.

"Ruby Jane Waskom, what have you two been doing? Dear Lord, you two can't be running around all hours like this in your underpants out in public. People will start talking. All of Knobby Waters will be gossiping about us and our house of ill repute. I got my good name to think of. My reputation. What will the single men think?"

I was too tuckered to point out to Sassy the hypocrisy of her concern. "Well," I said, as I moved toward the screen door, "I imagine the single men will be lined up around the house come morning. In my worldly experience—most of it gleamed from watching you all these years—a half-naked woman is one of the few things men in these parts pay any mind to. That and catfish."

Melvin laughed.

Sassy did not.

Veenie was storming around the kitchen pulling snacks out of the cupboard when I came in and plopped down in a chair. She'd piled the table high with a box of Twinkies, some pork cracklings, and a quart of chocolate milk.

I yanked a jar of Tums out of the cabinet to complete the feast.

We sat together sucking the crème out of Twinkies, not even turning the lights on.

We theorized about Darnell and the Gremlin being out at the mansion.

"What you reckon he was doing out there?" Veenie asked

"Must have been him digging around, making all those holes in the apple orchard."

"But we saw what looked like two ghostly figures and lights. Anyway, that's what I thought I saw with Boots's binoculars, but sometimes I don't see so well. That what you saw too?"

"Yep. Two figures."

"I dunno. Randy Ollis and his kin have kept that story about buried treasure alive all these generations. Must be something to a tale that lives that long."

Veenie gulped down a stream of chocolate milk. "Could be they're just like everybody else. Don't want to be poor and common. Like most folks in these parts, they don't have a lot to be proud of. All they got is that story. At least somebody in the family was famous once, even if it was for being a crazy polecat."

I heard footsteps tread up the basement stairs. The door sprung open, and Junior fell into the room. "Thought I heard you two yacking. What you doing up so late?" He was wearing a short velour robe over his underpants. His chest hair was fuzzed up like the tail end of a red squirrel. His John Lennon glasses rode low on his nose as he peered into the ice box. He pulled out a box of leftover Papa John's pizza and sat down at the table with us. He tore at the cold crust with his incisor teeth.

Veenie pulled a skin of cold cheese off the top of the pizza.

I updated Junior on the action with the Feds, the two recovered gold coins, and the news on Darnell's ancestry and arrest warrants.

"Oh man," he mumbled through pizza crust. "Seemed like such a decent guy too. Real free with the weed. Generous. You mean, it was like him who stole my hog, and you, Mama, who snatched it back?"

Veenie shrugged. "I know how hard you worked to get that bike."

Junior put the pizza down and gave his mama a bear hug.

That made Veenie spit and spatter a good bit.

I asked Junior if he'd seen Darnell or had any idea where Darnell might be hiding out in the Gremlin.

"Nah. Man, if I knew where that sticky-fingered, little fart was I'd be out there beating the weeds after him."

"Why?"

"Cause my guitars are missing. Some of my audio equipment too." He stopped and grabbed another slice of cold pizza.

"The Fender?"

"Yeah. Knowing what a crook he is, I reckon he took my stuff. Man, you just can't trust anybody these days." He inhaled the last of the pizza and stumbled back down the stairs.

Chapter Twenty-Nine

B y the time I rolled out of bed and washed the crust out of my eyes Veenie was in the kitchen stabbing at a pie and knocking back a pot of coffee with Dickie.

Dickie offered me a fat slice of cherry pie. "That one of Ma's pies?"

"Sure is," said Dickie. "Picked it up fresh on my way down the knobs. Brought the Chevy back. She's purring like a kitten. You gals could race that old heap in the 500, if you wanted."

I took the pie, poured myself a cup of dark coffee, and sat down to breakfast.

Veenie said Dickie knew the whereabouts of the purple Gremlin.

I almost choked on my coffee. "Where?"

"Seen it parked up on the knobs. Lover's Overlook," said Dickie.

"By the old dump?"

"Yep. It was up there about an hour ago when I rolled down the knobs giving the Chevy's brakes the old test drive."

"Was there a tent sticking out the back?"

"Sure. Canvas thing."

"You see any sign of a sloppy guy with a beard?"

"Nah. It was all quiet. The windows were fogged over with dew. It was pulled in under some oak trees. Why you asking?" Dickie swigged his coffee.

Veenie filled Dickie in on Darnell. How he'd stolen the Gremlin and was wanted for skipping bail. How he'd been digging around out at the mansion.

Dickie pushed the green seed cap back on his head. "You gals ought to send Boots up there to get Darnell. I don't like the thought of you two messing with the likes of that fellow."

Veenie shrugged. "We mess with the likes of Darnell every day. Heck I was married and all messed up with something worse than Darnell. And I'm all fine and dandy now."

"You was younger then, Lavinia."

"Sweet of you to say, Dickie."

The smooching started in.

I buried my head in a second piece of pie.

Dickie laid the keys to the Impala on the table and said he had to scoot. "Promised Bud I'd help him toss some hay before the heavens part and it rains. See you gals later."

As soon as Dickie was gone Veenie told me she had a plan. "We need to make payroll, right?"

"Technically, that's Harry's job. He's *supposed* to pay us."

"Like I said, *we* need to make payroll. We wait on Harry, we'll be eating our three squares off the free sample tables at the Costco."

She had a point. "What's your plan?"

"Darnell is worth a couple of big ones."

"If we get him to the Salem jail over in Washington County."

"His bail money would cover our next payroll."

"Sure would."

"So, I was thinking we take a drive up to the top of the knobs."

"The old dump?"

Veenie nodded.

"Darnell is a pretty big guy. Won't we need more muscle?"

"He's fat. He'll be stoned. Once we get him down, he'll be like a penguin. He'll never get back up on his own. I could sit

171

on him. You could twisty-tie his hands. We could shove him into the Gremlin. Deliver him all trussed up over to the fuzz in Washington County."

It sounded easy enough. And maybe it would have been easy, but by the time we got to the top of the knobs, the Gremlin had vanished. We could see its tracks in the mud. Darnell had left behind some PBR beer cans and a bag of trash, but the car and the man were nowhere to be found.

Veenie and I consoled ourselves by stopping at Ma Horton's pie shed and sharing a blueberry crumble for brunch. We ate it right there in the Impala, the doors wide open, listening to the chickens cluck. Dewey, the rooster, was perched high up in a pawpaw tree, crowing like he was Godzilla with tail feathers. The pie was still warm, so it slid down easily. Cheered us both up a good bit.

Veenie asked why we didn't just live on pie.

I said we ought to give it a try and got another pie to go from the shed, apple this time.

We were just fixing to drive down to the office and check in with Harry—maybe he'd found us some work—when I got a text. It was from snot-nosed Pooter Johnson.

"I know where Darnell is. Share reward?"

I thumbed back, "Maybe. Where are you?"

"Meet me in library parking lot."

I showed Veenie the screen, and she nodded. "Why not?"

I fired up the Impala and we were at the library chawing with Pooter in no time

Pooter hitched up his shorts. He straddled his banana seat bicycle and leaned precariously into the open window of the Impala. He was bare-chested with a bad sunburn on his shoulders and nose. He was doing his best to convince me and Veenie to give him a cash reward up front in exchange for the whereabouts of Darnell Zikes and his Gremlin.

Veenie said "No deal, punk."

Pooter pushed off the Impala. He popped a wheelie in the lot, then came back and leaned onto the car again. "I thought old ladies was sweet."

"That is her being sweet," I said. "Normally she has the personality of a porcupine."

"Look," cried Pooter, "all I want is a hundred bucks. I watch TV. Snitches get paid. You find Darnell, and you'll make some sweet bucks. I'm asking for a little cut. A commission. Not being greedy nor nothing, just trying to make an honest buck. You want to deal or what?"

Boots cruised by and flipped his cherry and whooper at us but then kept right on rolling.

Veenie said we could guarantee a C-note, but only if we caught Darnell and got our full reward.

Pooter hemmed and hawed. "How you gonna bring in a big fellow like that?"

"We got our ways. Besides, his brain's not all that big. He's ass, mostly."

"Shake on it?" Pooter thrust his dirty little hand into the Chevy's window and reached across the front seat toward Veenie.

Veenie gave him a high five.

Ten minutes later, we were out by the river at the turnoff to the Moon Glo Motor Lodge. We'd thrown Pooter's bike in the trunk and given him a ride out.

"There he is," Pooter said. "Just like I said." Pooter pointed straight ahead toward the covered bridge.

The purple top of the Gremlin was visible in the weeds, not far from the Moon Glo's front office. The dimwit had parked in almost the exact same spot as before. The hatchback was down. The tent gone. The front driver's door, which faced away from us, was open. It looked like someone was hanging out the door smoking, maybe getting some fresh air in the car. Smoke curled above the door.

Veenie and I eyed each other as Pooter spun away on his bike. "Later, grannies," he yelled, not waiting around to offer assistance.

"I'll take the passenger's side," I said.

Veenie grabbed her BB pistol out of the glove compartment and stuck it in the waistband of her capris. "Let's roll, Louise."

Chapter Thirty

Darnell didn't look surprised to see us. He sat in the driver's bucket seat with his chubby legs dangling out the door. He was barefoot. He had on a wife beater T-shirt and some pale blue boxers. His pigtails were coming unraveled. He was toking on a doobie. He squinted when Veenie demanded he put up his hands.

"Can't," he explained. "Gotta finish this doobie. Want some? Sweet stuff. Dream potion number nine." He held it out to Veenie.

She poked him under the right eye with the barrel tip of the BB gun.

"Ouch! Just so you know, that hurt, Granny."

"Sit still or I'll shoot your eyes out."

I could see Junior's Fender guitar and a pile of mics and drums in the back seat of the Gremlim. That did not surprise me. What did surprise me was what erupted out of the pile of dirty blankets next to the musical paraphernalia.

Kandy Huggins.

"Oh shit!" said Kandy, and she dove back under the covers.

Veenie said, "We came to get Junior's stuff."

"Oh man, is that his stuff?" Darnell looked over his shoulder. His forehead was lined with wrinkles. "Oh shit, didn't mean to take his stuff. I guess I was stoned. You can have anything you like. Take anything. We'll call it square."

Veenie kept the gun pressed to the bottom socket of his right eye. "You stole this car too."

"Oh man, did I? You know, I think I got a problem. I think I might be an addict. I've been having these blackouts. You know, I was an abused kid. It was awful. So awful I got to drink and do drugs just to keep from killing myself some days. I'm not as happy go lucky as I look, you know."

Veenie said, "Tell it to your parole officer."

"Oh man, come on! You're not taking me in, are you? Me and you are friends. Can't you just take Junior's stuff and look the other way? I was on my way out of town. I'll be gone soon as you get your stuff. You'll never see me again. Why make a fuss?"

Kandy peeked out of the covers. "Come on gals, we were just leaving town. Weren't nobody hurt. Everybody had fun."

I told Kandy we knew about her arrest warrant for running scams over in Missouri.

"Oh Jesus," she said. "I'm an entertainer. That's all. People used to love being entertained. I never hurt nobody. Me and Darnell, we're a team."

"A team?"

Darnell took another toke. "She's my wife."

"Ex-wife!" Kandy screeched. "Ex!"

"You two were in this ghost swindle together?"

Darnell objected. "I never invited her to come down here with me."

Kandy rolled her eyes. "Like I was going to let you get your hands on that gold and not give me my fair share. He owes me ten years of alimony, you know."

Somehow that did not surprise me.

Kandy yacked on. "He'd been going on about his big family jewels ever since I met him in the carnival down in Kentucky. Yack. Yack. Yack. How his great-great-granddad was a big old train and bank robber. How someday he was going to find the loot and we'd be rich."

I asked Darnell how he knew he was related to Alta Iona.

"Did one of them spit tests. Mailed it in online. They tell you if you're related to anyone famous. Thought it might come in handy, knowing some relatives I could stay with when I was down and out. Thought I might even find some wealthy kin and show up asking for some cousin money and consideration. Alta Iona came up on my mama's side, along with an old news story on the missing gold. Did some digging in the library. Found more details about the gold at the Wyatt mansion. Used the story mostly to impress the ladies."

Kandy made a funny sound. "What? You think he lured me in with his charm?"

Darnell shrugged that off. "Anyway, Kandy said we could run the ghost racket. See what the neighbors knew. Get in on the inside track. I decided to come on up this way. When you ladies got involved and I saw that piece in the *Squealer* on the skeleton, I called Kandy to come up, get on the inside with you gals. Get everybody's confidence so I could get on with digging around for the gold."

Veenie eyed Kandy. "That why you were smooching up Harry?"

"That and the fact he's kind of cute. Like a baby otter with that itty-bitty moustache of his."

Veenie and I both winced.

Darnell finished his doobie and flicked it off into the weeds. "You're gonna let us go, right?"

"Wrong," said Veenie. "There are warrants for the both of you. I figure we can trade you two in for enough cash to keep us in Twinkies until Christmas."

Kandy said, "I am not going to the slammer. You know what that would do to my hair?"

Right now her hay pile of hair was full of rats' nests. I imagined prison could only improve it.

Out of curiosity, I asked if they ever found any gold.

Kandy snorted. "Heck no! We did a lot of digging. All we ever got was blisters. I was hanging around trying to make a little cash for the road doing ghost shows for Dode. At least he had some cash."

"Whatever made you think there was gold in the apple orchard?"

"Ask the genius there." Kandy pointed to Darnell.

"Here, I'll show you." Darnell asked Veenie to lower the BB gun.

She did—reluctantly.

He reached over and pulled his fat biker's wallet out of the console. He unfolded a piece of paper. It looked like an old plate ripped out of a book. "When Alta Iona left my great-great-granny, Myrtle Mae, at the orphanage, all she left with her was this here page out of a bible."

Veenie and I studied the page. It looked to be a scene from some old painting. A curly-haired maiden in long flowing robes had her arms sprawled out wide. She held an apple tree branch with three fat, ripe apples that glinted like gold. Under the picture someone had written in ink, "Under the three apples, not on the tree. On the word of God, that's where the gold will be." The initials AIW were scribbled under the inscription.

Darnell sniveled. "I reckoned Alta Iona wrote this—AIW, see?—and that it meant she'd hidden Jedidiah's stolen gold in the apple orchard. I reckoned she hoped whoever got the baby would understand the message. Get the gold so little Myrtle Mae would be taken care of right nice."

Kandy snorted. "I told him that story he made up in his head about golden apples was far-fetched."

"Hey! A guy can dream."

"I wish you would. Go for it. For heaven's sake, you steal a car—a felony, I might add—and do you steal a Caddy or something hot and sexy like what rich people would drive? Oh no, you steal a Gremlin. A '73 purple Gremlin, for the love of God Almighty."

Darnell's face fell a little. "I think it's cute."

Veenie shook her BB gun. "If you two are done bellyaching, we're taking you in. Move it. Over to the Chevy."

Darnell shuffled out of the Gremlin. He looked down at his bare, chubby legs "I need some pants," he said. "Kandy!" he called to the back seat. "Throw me them pants over by the cooler."

Kandy dove down. When she popped back up, her hands were no longer empty. They didn't hold pants either. She was gripping a sawed-off shotgun. And not an air pistol either. "Sorry, gals," she said. "Kandy Huggins is not going to the big house. Not even for one itty-bitty night. Hand over your pistol and your cell phones."

Veenie and I complied.

Kandy ordered Darnell to get some rope out of the Gremlin. He tied us up sitting on the ground, back-to-back. Then he hog-tied our ankles. Kandy fished the Chevy keys out of my front pocket. The pair took off in the Impala, headed south toward the state line.

"On the bright side," I said, as I leaned back into Veenie. "We did get Junior's guitar back. And we got the Gremlin. Bet there's a reward for that Gremlin." I nodded toward the car. "Also, the Impala is low on gas. They probably won't make it to the state line."

It was almost dark when Boots slid into the sand next to us.

He mashed on his hat and moseyed on over to us. "Well, well," he said, trying his darnedest not to crack a grin. "You gals need a ride home, do you?"

Chapter Thirty-One

Harry was happy to have his stereo and big screen TV back in his apartment. Also, his bottle of good Kentucky bourbon. All the stuff Kandy had stolen from him had been stuffed in the Gremlin. He had it all back now.

"I knew that Kandy was putting me on," Harry said. He leaned back in his chair, put his feet up on the desk and lit a cigarette. He inhaled deeply, then took a shot of bourbon. He loosened his tie, then took another shot of bourbon.

"Yeah," said Veenie. "You sure was on top of that one."

Darnell and Kandy had listed all Harry's stuff on Craigslist, but none of it had moved. I could kind of see why. The whiskey was top shelf, but the rest of the stuff looked like Harry had gotten it at a fire sale at the Big Lots.

Veenie said that was because Harry *had* gotten it at a fire sale at the Big Lots.

We were all moping around the office. We were pretty much back to where we started. Dead broke. No new cases. The guy who owned the Gremlin didn't even want the car back. Said we could keep it as a finder's fee. Dickie said he could fix it up, probably sell it for us for a cool thousand over at Sammy Spray's All-American Auto Lot. I couldn't think of anything more all-American than a Gremlin. Some hipster was bound to buy it. Everything vintage was hot these days. Everybody wanted the seventies back. Everybody but we oldsters who survived it the first time around. I was in no hurry to bring back the seventies. Pantyhose were big back then.

Being tall and lanky, I stumbled around for an entire decade with my crotch down around my knees.

Junior had his band equipment back. I reckoned that was good. It would have been tragic if the Lip Lizards had not been able to pluck and twang at Pokey's anymore. We were able to tell Pokey that Darnell was the one who had been stealing the mystery meat and beer from the back room. Not that it helped, but it did get Pokey to put a new lock on the back alley window, and it did earn us free mystery meat sandwiches for the rest of our lives, which as far as Veenie was concerned was better than cash money.

We didn't get much else out of the whole escapade. All we had in the end was the page Darnell's had ripped from some book, three golden apples on it. "What do you reckon this means?" I asked Veenie.

She shrugged and read the inscription out loud. "Under the three apples, not on the tree. On the word of God, that's where the gold will be."

Harry took a look. "Looks like one of those pages they used to put in family bibles. My great aunt had one of those big old family bibles. Had the family tree in the middle. Some fancy pages to record births and deaths. Some of the Bible stories were illustrated like this. People couldn't read much back in the day, so books had a lot of these pictures. Don't imagine it means anything. Just some tall tale."

"I dunno," said Veenie. "Alta Iona was a new mama. Probably loved that baby something fierce. Probably hated that old Jedidiah just as much."

I studied the illustration. "Must be a story behind this. Maybe Queet over at the library would recognize the picture as some sort of ancient art or as a picture from a Bible story."

I asked Harry if he had any work for us.

"Nah." He'd almost drained his bottle of bourbon.

"Mind if we kick off early?"

"As long as you don't expect to be paid for the day. I'm not paying for lollygagging."

With the Impala stolen, Veenie and I were back to go-karting. "Come on," I said to Veenie. "Let's go see Queet at the library, get you some more old lady smut to read."

● ● ●

Queet was delighted to see us. She was crawling around in the fiction department, re-shelving. She got up and swept the wavy hair out of her eyes. "Heard your old Impala got stolen."

"Figure they'll find it eventually. Not likely Kandy and Darnell will outrun the law in that car. It runs fine and dandy until you hit sixty. Then it trembles like Moses meeting his maker."

"So the whole ghost thing out at the Wyatt mansion, that was all fake?"

"Pretty much. It was Darnell and his ex-wife, that medium we hired, digging around for Jedidiah's gold."

"Darnell was kin to Jedidiah Wyatt?"

"He's an Ollis. Great-great-grandson to Alta Iona. Found it out using one of them family trace DNA databases."

"Amazing what they can tell from a bit of spit, eh? No gold out there then?"

"Not that anyone ever found. The Feds got those two coins Dode had stashed in his money jars."

"Confederate money. Worth half a million. Can you beat that? I bet Dode is sorting through his spare change more carefully now. He remember where he got those coins?"

"Nah. He always threw his change into those jars. Those coins could have been in those jars for fifty years. In any case, Veenie and I got zippo, except for this page out of a book. It's signed by Alta Iona. She left it at the orphanage with Myrtle Mae."

Queet took the page and slipped on her reading glasses, which hung on a chain around her neck. "Hmm. This looks mighty familiar. Wait here just a minute."

I had nowhere else to go, so I plopped down in a reading chair.

Veenie was already engrossed in a large print Father Mackie romance novel.

I thumbed through some magazines, then scanned the county paper for Hoosier Feedbag coupons.

A couple of minutes later, Queet motioned for us to come into the conference room behind the checkout counter. She was set up thumbing through a tattered cardboard box of stuff. It was the same box we'd sifted through before with Queet—the Ollis family box. I recognized the photos of Jedidiah and Alta spread out on the table. There was also a stack of yellowed papers. Queet lifted a book out of the box and slid it over to me. "Alta's Bible," she said.

The Bible was huge, thick as a cement block. Its black leather cover was cracked. The front was embossed with Alta's name in gold.

Queet tapped the book. "I think your apple print came out of this Bible. There's a page missing near the middle. Ripped out. Let me see your page again."

I handed Queet the page. She held it up against a ripped edge inside the Bible. "Fits like a glove. See."

She was right. "But what's it mean?"

Queet shrugged. "There are plates all through this Bible. That one seems to be about the Garden of Eden."

"The old devil apple story, eh?"

"Appears to be."

"Why would Alta write that inscription on it?"

"Got me. I don't recognize that inscription as any known poem."

"So it was a personal message? Meant for whoever took Myrtle Mae in and raised her?"

"Might be." Queet lifted the Bible and placed it back in the box. "Guess we'll never know."

My cell phone was vibrating. It was a call from Dode.

"Got something for you, missy," he said. "You anywhere out this way?"

"Give me twenty minutes. I could be."

"Well, gosh darn, come on over. I got some chicken and dumplings warming on the stove. My sister dropped off a fresh pot for me. Be glad to share."

He didn't have to repeat that offer.

Chapter Thirty-Two

V eenie shoveled into her bowl of chicken and dumplings.
I pretty much did the same.

We were sitting around the table in Dode's kitchen. The place was neat as a pin. He had a cute little table cloth with bluebirds flying around the hemline and curtains to match. The place smelled like warm tasty chicken. We'd stopped at the pie shed and brought Dode an apple crumble from Ma Horton to complete the dinner.

Veenie finished her chicken and dumplings and asked for seconds.

"Help yourself," said Dode. "Lick the pot clean."

I asked Dode if his sister brought him dinner often.

"Once a week, most weeks. She lives over in Tunnelton. Widowed. Gardens a little. Makes her pocket money growing organic herbs for bigwig professors at the university. Has a little side business making apple butter in the fall. Comes over and gathers up apples from the Wyatt orchard. Stores them here in my cellar until she's ready to cook 'em down. Keeps her busy all winter. Been doing that her whole life. Whips up a mean persimmon pudding too. They pay her to bring batches over to the old folks' home."

Dode dabbed at his chin with a napkin. "That's mighty fine pie," he said. "Can't beat that." He forked the rest of the pie into his mouth, then jiggered out a second piece.

I asked Dode why he wanted to see us.

"Oh yeah, almost forgot." He grinned like a kid. "Wait here, missy. I'll be right back."

He crab-walked out of the kitchen and down the hall. I heard some shuffling. He loped back in and held something out in his outstretched hand. It was a personal check for five thousand dollars.

"What's this for, Dode?"

"You and Miss Lavinia."

"You already paid us. The retainer. The money jars. Remember?"

"Oh sure, but this here money is from the government. Your share."

"Our share of what?"

"You found them gold coins. The government pays a tidy recovery fee for stolen merchandise long as a feller signs a release saying he won't make no claim on the stolen property or against the government. That there is your half. I figured I owed you this much. I got some too. Gonna use mine to buy a new squirrel rifle. Put some tires on the tractor."

Veenie inspected the check. "Hot diggity. I'm going to buy me a whole new summer outfit. Something new and classy from the Walmart, maybe even hit the Costco."

"Dode, you sure you want us to have this money?"

"Sure am. You earned it. I ain't had so much fun since I was a kid in short pants. What with the ghosts and the medium, and all. Most folks don't pay me no mind, but you gals showed me a real good time."

Veenie piped up. "We had a great time too, didn't we Ruby Jane?"

"Yep. The best."

I wondered what Dode thought about all the buried treasure stories. "You reckon Jedidiah buried all that Confederate gold out here?"

"Don't rightly know. Wish I could remember where I found those Confederate coins, but shucks I don't. Probably found them when I was a kid. I've been stashing money away most all my life."

"We were wondering if maybe there was more gold out here."

"What makes you all think that?"

I showed Dode the print from the Bible with the hand-written message from Alta. "Under the three apples, not on the tree. On the word of God, that's where the gold will be." I asked if the inscription meant anything to him.

He nodded no, but took the page and stuck it up closer to his face. "No, them words don't mean much to me. But I know that picture."

"The woman with the three apples?"

"Yep. Sure do."

"You seen that picture before?"

"Sure. Lots of times. It's carved in a stone, out back in my apple cellar."

"Can you show us?"

He forked down the last of the apple pie. "Don't see why not."

• • •

Veenie and I stared at each other in disbelief. We were standing at the threshold of Dode's apple cellar, out behind his farmhouse. The cellar was at least one hundred years old. It was built into the side of a natural embankment. The front was curved like the top of a beehive. The walls were constructed of stacked slabs of lichen-crusted limestone. Plant and tree roots crawled in tangles along the limestone wall. The door was fashioned of weathered boards lashed together, with an iron pull ring as a handle.

I asked Dode how long the cellar had been there.

"Don't rightly know." He lifted the black seed cap on his head, put it back down. "Long as the house, I expect. Granny Schneider kept blue john milk and cream out here. I just keep apples, persimmons, root vegetables. Extra jars of pickles and beets and three bean salad my sister cans for me. Some zucchini relish. Got a natural cold spring runs inside. Come on in. I'll give you a peek."

Dode creaked open the door. The bottom of the door scraped the mud and stone floor, but he managed to get it leveraged back. He kicked a stone against it so it would hold open. A spray of light from the pole light out by the barn lit up the interior of the cellar.

We stepped over the threshold stone of Eve with the three golden apples. The cellar ceiling was made of mud and roots. Dode and I had to stoop and duckwalk to make it in, but Veenie strolled in like a Keebler elf. A pocked limestone trough ran along the back wall where water trickled into the cave-like structure. Dode pulled a penlight out of the pencil pocket on the bib of his coveralls and flashed it around the interior. Moldy boards held together by rusty nails lined the right side of the cellar. Dode took the flat of his hand and swept away cobwebs so Veenie and I could step farther into the depths of the cellar. It smelled like a cave.

Dode pointed to the far corner of the cellar, where two muddy holes were filling with spring water. "That's where I kept my money jars."

"You come out here much?" I asked.

"Nah. Just to get canned goods in the early winter to tide me over. My sister comes in here in the fall to squirrel away apples. Not much in the bins now. Too early. Come September this cellar will be busting with apples. She stores them over yonder in the metal-lined bins. Keeps them cool. Keeps the critters from gnawing on them."

I walked back to the door and stared at the threshold stone. The woman with the three golden apples was the same as on the Bible etching. She'd probably been carved into the limestone by one of the quarry masons over in Bedford or Oolitic. The stone looked tightly set in the doorway.

"Pretty, ain't it?" said Dode. He flashed his penlight across the stone.

Veenie strolled over and stared at the stone with me. "You ever look under that stone, Dode?"

"Can't rightly recall." He danced the light across the apples. "You reckon I should?"

Chapter Thirty-Three

Dode fired up the tractor. He fastened a grappling hook over the ends of the threshold stone to drag it up out of place. The stone had been ground deep into the clay. Once the hook bit into the limestone, Dode gunned the tractor. The stone slid easily up and out of place across the wet greasy grass.

Melvin was there, down on his hunches, watching the excavation. I'd called him to keep things on the up-and-up. Veenie had wanted to keep the excavation on the down low, but that gold—if it was there—belonged to the US Treasury, and I wasn't about to end up bunking alongside the likes of Darnell and Kandy in the big house on grand larceny theft charges.

Melvin was all dandied up in gray slacks and a gentleman's light blue sweater, per usual. He borrowed some duck boots from Dode so he didn't get his expensive tasseled loafers ruined in the muddy ground around the spring.

We'd called Harry in too, just because, well, he was the boss. He'd been slinking around like a spanked puppy since Kandy had whipped his ass and took him for a ride. I figured if there were gold under that stone, it might cheer him up a bit. It might even put him in a good enough humor to sign our paychecks for the week. I had my eye on a new goose down pillow over at the Farmer's Market. Thirty bucks cash, and it'd be mine.

When the stone slid away, we were all disappointed not to see any shiny gold.

Melvin duckwalked closer and held up his hand for us to wait a minute. He took a long, flat-head screwdriver out of the utility tray on Dode's tractor and starting poking in the clay. It wasn't long before we heard a rattling sound. He'd hit metal. A couple of pokes later and he had a rust-riddled tobacco tin pulled up onto the grass.

In a way, Alta Iona really had been haunting the Wyatt homestead. Under the threshold stone she had left not only the Confederate gold but also a handwritten letter, sealed in wax inside a metal Red Injun tobacco tin.

Melvin unfolded the letter, careful not to crumble it in his grip. The letter was a bit moldy with a worm hole or two. He had to hold it up to the light from the barn poles to read it aloud to us. It was addressed to "Dear Gentle People," and talked about the Confederate gold. Alta Iona had meant for the gold to be used for her baby's care and upbringing.

The letter outlined how heartbroken she was that Jedidiah, whom she had loved, had taken her family's hard-won fortune and left her, the baby, and everyone else in the town destitute. The letter explained how she felt poorly during her pregnancy. Even worse after they took the baby away. Food ran through her. She was dizzy. She saw demons swinging in the apple orchard. She couldn't feed or care for the baby in even the simplest way, so she had, heartbroken, allowed her brother Jeb to place the girl child in an orphanage.

The rest, she wrote, was up to the Lord God to make right someday.

April, the coroner, who'd also come out for the excavation, confirmed that Alta's symptoms were consistent with a slow death through arsenic poisoning. She shook her head, sad as we all were to hear the story. "Jedidiah probably added the poison to Alta's food in small quantities for a good while before she took deathly sick. His goal had likely been to make sure Alta didn't have the wits about her to see that she and the town were being robbed blind. Alta would have felt like she had the flu. Eventually grew so weak she couldn't hold anything down in her stomach. Would have hallucinated a good bit at the end, poor woman."

Apparently Alta had been lucid long enough to find and hide the Confederate gold from Jedidiah. If he ever did come back looking for his stolen fortune, it was safely hidden under the cellar stone. County records confirmed that originally the cellar had been on Jedidiah's acreage. Alta must have commissioned the threshold stone because she loved that illustration in the family Bible. She was betting Jedidiah, that old hound dog, would never open the Bible or pay much mind to any of the scriptures, keeping her message safe for more righteous eyes.

It was a unique hiding place, a place not likely to ever be disturbed or dug through by accident. She couldn't have imaged how cellars and springhouses would come to be replaced with indoor ice chests. Over the decades, with no one to claim the Wyatt homestead, the Schneiders had adopted a liberal view of property boundaries. They started making use of the cellar and the apples as their own.

After the press got wind of the gold, Darnell appeared on TV in his pigtails, sniffling, saying the letter was proof that he ought to be getting all the gold as his rightful inheritance. He opened an online account asking people to fund his legal fees. He and Kandy had not gotten far in the Impala. They'd run out of gas on the Sparksville iron bridge and been picked up by the Washington County authorities. Because they both had extensive records, they looked to be headed for a long stint in the slammer.

For a few days after the gold was found, press vans and reporters crawled like fire ants all over Knobby Waters. Harry squeezed himself into every photo. He bought a new hat and some cigars. He handed out his business cards like penny candy.

Randy Ollis found himself on the TV talk shows, telling his family story time and again. He was happy as a squirrel with a nest of nuts to be the focus of so much attention. The money from the talk show appearances allowed him to upgrade to a new trailer and pickup truck.

Some of Squeal Daddy's blog posts and insider photos went national.

Harry didn't see why he ought to share the Confederate gold with anyone. "The Shades Agency found that gold. I own the Shades Agency. Heck, I *am* the Shades Agency," he told the TV cameras. He puffed up a good bit when he said that.

Melvin Beal disagreed. "That gold is stolen federal property. It belongs to the US Treasury. Of course, if you prefer, Harry, we could get a busload of lawyers down here and some nosey fellows from the IRS.

"The IRS?" Harry clutched his lapels. "Why would we need them?"

"They like to look into things like this. Sudden cash windfalls and all."

Harry considered his options. "I get a finder's fee, don't I?"

Melvin said that could be arranged. The town would get a share too, since some of the money was tied to their being swindled, but a full settlement might take a bit. The Confederate gold was rumored to be worth more than ten million dollars all total, but since nothing like this had ever been found before, its full value was uncertain.

Melvin also reminded Harry that the gold was not likely to be sold. It was a part of America's great Civil War history. It would likely end up in the Smithsonian or some other government museum on display so everybody could enjoy it.

Sassy loved that she got to sashay around town on the arm of a good-looking federal agent all week. She cut out the pictures of her and Melvin that appeared in the news and pinned them to one of her wish boards. She kept what she called these "vision boards." Her walls were covered with them. She said they portrayed her life the way it ought to be, not the common way she'd been forced to live lately since her last husband went up the river for some harebrained real estate scheme. Unfortunately Melvin was called back to DC when the case was closed. Sassy slid back to living the common life with the rest of us old geezers in Knobby Waters.

While Harry was busy grand standing on the national news, Veenie and I returned to work. We felt a whole lot richer than we'd ever been. Dode's five-thousand-dollar gift to us was a heap of money. We were dining like queens on an unlimited supply of free mystery meat sandwiches, and we had the Impala back. Dickie towed the Impala back to Knobby Waters from the Washington County impound down in Salem once we could prove it was ours and not involved in any interstate crime.

As a special gift to Veenie, he installed an eight-track tape player he got free at a local barn auction. The player came with a box of mint condition eight-track tapes. Really good stuff too: Dolly Parton, Johnny Cash, Lester Flatt and Earl Scruggs, and The Eagles. Now Veenie and I could crank tunes while tooling around town crime-busting.

All of this just in time too.

Down in Hound Holler, on the other side of the knobs, trouble was boiling up. It involved Shap Reynolds and his Combine of Death, and more than one fellow doing the dance with no pants with the wrong lady friend …

Read On to begin the *Baby Daddy Mystery, The Shady Hoosier Detective Agency: Book 2.*

Chapter One

The windows of the detective agency rattled like God's wind chimes as Shap Reynolds thundered by on his Combine of Death. Shap had been driving up and down Main Street all morning, honking at the agency, screaming death threats at Harry Shades, our boss. Shap looked mighty put out. His normally pasty-white face was red as a watermelon, and his blue eyes, normally as quiet as a summer sky, were shaking in his head. He had more spittle and sweat running down his face than a boxer dog gone mad.

I'd been trying all morning to ignore Shap. I had my head down, my whole body hunched over my computer keyboard. I wasn't getting a lick of work done because of the road racket and Shap's shouting. Clearly, the old coot felt he'd been wronged, and he wasn't going back to his farming until somebody paid him some mind.

Veenie, on the other hand, was sitting next to me, sympathizing with the brokenhearted old fart. She peered up over her thick glasses. "Harry been diddling Shap's wife, Dottie, again?"

"That'd be my guess."

"Why you reckon he keeps hitting on that? You ask me, she looks like the type of gal he'd be best off renting by the hour."

"She was Miss Starlite Bowling," I reminded Veenie.

"Back in the seventies."

"The heart wants what the heart wants."

Veenie thumped the return on her keyboard. "Looks to me like a heap of other organs might have gotten involved."

Lavinia Goens—Veenie—is my best pal. She's seventy-one years old with a chipmunk face and a white wisp of kewpie doll hair. Her blue eyes twinkle like stars behind her Coke bottle glasses. People think she's a little doll, until she opens her pie hole. Most days she itches for excitement with so much energy she practically bounces around the office.

My name is Ruby Jane Waskom—RJ to most—and at the age of sixty-seven, I itch for a weekly paycheck. Veenie and I have been best pals since we worked side by side on the auto button line at the Bold Mold Plastics Factory. This was way back, before the EPA decided that pouring plastic waste into White River was a doo-doo of an idea.

The Harry Shades Detective Agency, where we work now, had received a passel of threatening phone calls from Shap earlier that morning. In his defense, Shap had good reason to be barking at us. That reason was not me. It was not Veenie. It was our boss, Harry Shades, private eye, and champion man skank. It was Spring in Knobby Waters, Indiana, and Harry, like most of God's creatures, had been busy rattling the sheets.

The last time Shap caught Harry dicky dunkin' his wife, he'd sprayed our office with a 20 gauge. Veenie wanted to leave the scatter holes visible. This being a detective agency, and all, she thought it added "atmosphere." I thought it'd scare the poop out of our clients, most of whom were not all that eager to be on the receiving end of a buckshot shower.

Harry's affair with Dottie Reynolds was seasonal—a perennial, I reckon you'd call it. Shap tried to mow Harry down with his combine last Spring. You'd think Harry would have learned his lesson, but oh no, like Dewey, Ma Horton's prize rooster, he was back on the strut. Not wanting to be reaped and threshed by Shap, Harry, who lived upstairs above the office, shimmied out the alley window early this morning. He tore out of town. If history repeated itself, he'd be gone about a week, two weeks tops. Harry liked Dottie, and he loved sex, but he wasn't about to die for either of them.

"Harry here?" Veenie asked. She'd come in late—stopped to watch the Widow Guthrie shooting noisy, lust-puffed woodpeckers off the lip of her grain elevator—and had missed the circus of phone calls.

"Skedaddled. Said the place was ours."

"On a bender?" Veenie loved saying "bender." She loved to pretend that we lived on the set of *Dragnet* instead of tucked between cornfields in the soggy bottomlands of Indiana.

"On the lamb," I said. "Boy, I wish just once Harry would hang around and take his medicine like a man. Maybe we could get some work done. It's mighty hard concentrating on work with ding dongs like old Shap taking potshots at us."

Veenie peered up over her glasses. "Harry hiding out until the affair blows over?"

"Or Shap runs out of shotgun shells."

Harry Shades isn't a bad man, just not the brightest. He is on the right side of sixty and still wears the same size pants as in high school, same style too: wide-waist, rayon dress pants from Sears. He is a bowling prodigy, able to pick up pocket change and loose women with regularity at the Tuesday night Starlite Bowling for Dollars Extravaganza. He has all his hair, which is the color of pewter, and he wears three-piece suits. He is a catch, provided you aren't all that fussy about what lands on the end of your line. Why he only "dates" married women and skanks, only the good Lord knows. Likes the drama, I reckon.

Veenie printed documents and slid them into a "case closed" file folder. The Mellencamp case was done. We'd caught Mr. Newt Mellencamp cheating on his wife, Betty, with Conchita, the countywide Mary Kay cosmetics saleslady. Now everyone knew what a slime ball Newt was. He'd have to cough up alimony, maybe even an apology. Veenie and I both considered that a good week's work.

As you may have gathered, Veenie and I are detectives, or junior detectives as Harry likes to remind us. Harry got his PI license from one of those Internet colleges. He has a badge and a diploma. When Harry gets uppity—that would be a butt load of the time, folks—Veenie likes to remind him that his diploma, a teeny-weenie laminated thing that fits in his wallet, looks exactly like something Barbie might carry in her purse to a job interview.

Husbands with hanky-panky pants are the bread-and-butter of the Shades Detective Agency. (Known locally as the Shady Hoosier Detective Agency because of the boss's spotty reputation with the ladies). Most days our work is pretty humdrum. Veenie and I hunt down deadbeat dads and cheating spouses. Harry waves his gun around and shakes down the offenders for loose change. There is usually more than enough work to keep us in bologna and cheese. Heck, on a good week, we might even afford a Dairy Queen run.

One thing Pawpaw County has in spades is cheating heart Romeos. Over at the old folks' home, recently splashed with a fresh coat of yellow paint and renamed Leisure Hills—Ha! Like that fooled anyone—it is a downright badge of honor among old coots to die while in the manly throes of romance. Squeal Daddy, the anonymous blogger who runs the *Hoosier Squealer* website, loves penning lurid gossip about the number and type of "death boners" over at the old folks' home. Romantic injuries are also a favored topic of conversation down at the VFW. The VFW is the social hub of Knobby Waters, should you be over sixty and in need of some reasonably sane conversation—and cheap well drinks on Wednesdays.

Sliding aside the Mellencamp case file, Veenie popped open a drawer on her desk. Her tiny liver-spotted hands dangled a brown paper bag under my nose. "Made us some tuna fish."

I squinted at her. "You look slimmer. Tuna fish diet?"

"Nah. Got me some new old lady undies. Newfangled. Had a run of seconds down at the Goodwill." Veenie showed me the top waistband of her underwear. It was beige and read "Spankies."

By seconds, I hoped she meant irregulars.

"They help slim me up," said Veenie as she patted at the Spankies, "but they ain't Moses. Can't perform miracles."

Veenie is wider than she is tall. Four feet seven. One hundred fifty pounds. She likes to wear outfits she thinks disguises her beach ball physique, mostly capri stretch pants and ponchos. Ponchos had been easy enough to find in the early seventies but have fallen out of fashion in the greater Midwest in the last forty years. This does not deter Veenie. On a tight budget, she shops for clothes in the Goodwill dumpster in the alley between the Road Kill Café and the post office. She likes to get the good stuff before it gets pawed through by the public. If she finds anything worth snatching, she always leaves a two-dollar cash donation. Today's Goodwill steal was a zebra striped poncho and a pair of bumble bee yellow capris. Fetching.

I fished in the paper bag and yanked out a sandwich. It was wrapped in waxed paper. Yellow squished out the edges. "Mustard?"

"Yours has mustard. Course it does." Veenie nibbled at her sandwich. She washed it down with a carton of chocolate milk. "How long you think Harry will be gone?"

I shrugged and chomped on my tuna. "A week?" I pulled a lettuce leaf out from between my back molars. It was red, the kind I liked. I had another go at it.

With Harry on the lamb, Veenie and I ran the detective agency pretty much as we pleased. I wrote our weekly paychecks. Veenie tallied and replenished the petty cash. We

kept busy making Knobby Waters a respectable place to live—
or die, as the case might be. Our clients tended to be elderly or
heavy drinkers, or both.

We agreed that while Harry was out of town, we'd embrace
any soul who hocked up the five-hundred-dollar retainer. We
were all ears once we had the five big ones.

Taking cases indiscriminately was a decision we began to
regret right after lunch. The tuna was barely licked from our
fingers and Shap, convinced Harry had fled, had finally
wheeled out of town, when Avonelle Apple huffed through our
door.

Everybody in Knobby Waters knew Avonelle, the bank
president. She'd lived here her whole life, and she was the only
person in town with home-dyed hair the color of apricots.
Veenie, along with most of Pawpaw County, had been spitting
and spatting with Avonelle for the better part of fifty years.

Judging by the determined look on Avonelle's face as she
stormed into the office, I could tell that one heck of a new
battle was brewing.

Chapter Two

Avonelle's apricot-colored hair was puffed up like cotton candy. Her eyebrows, penciled on in high arches, were a darker shade of apricot. She wore a nice knit suit in a pastel green with a large white Buster Brown silk tie like the kind Nancy Reagan used to wear. She carried a black purse with a gold clasp with both hands, placing it dead-center across her lady parts. Overall, she was shaped like a bowling pin and had a personality pretty much the same.

Avonelle pulled out a monogrammed handkerchief and dusted off the seat I offered her. She sat down like a lady and crossed her ankles, then nervously uncrossed her ankles. She wiggled in the chair. It was a tight fit with those bowling-pin hips. She sighed deeply as if already put out with the Shades Detective Agency and whatever misfortune had forced her to darken our door.

Veenie, playing it safe, had vamoosed behind a file cabinet. I could hear her tiny ears flapping, trying to snatch every syllable of Avonelle's distress. Clearly Avonelle had a problem, and Veenie wasn't about to miss out on any ear-busting gossip.

A natural born judge, Avonelle appointed herself head of every town committee. That was how she and Veenie came to lock horns. Back in 1968, Avonelle had judged the cat contest at the Pawpaw County Fair. The way Veenie told it, Avonelle had cheated Veenie's calico cat, Mrs. Puff Pants, out of the grand champion ribbon. The award went instead to Mrs. Hall's tuxedo cat, Cary "Claws" Grant. In exchange, Mrs. Hall voted

Avonelle in as Grand Poobah of the Knobby Waters Ladies Home Improvement Society. That incident was the beginning of a fifty-year grudge.

"How might we help you?" I asked Avonelle as I plucked up a pen and a legal pad and smoothed down my halo of white hair. Avonelle seemed like a good bet as a client, so I did my darnedest to look professional. Everyone knew Avonelle had oodles of money. She'd inherited controlling stock in the First National Bank of Knobby Waters from her daddy. Her husband, Will, had been the town dentist. He was recently deceased. His twin sons inherited his practice. One of his cousins ran the denture lab over in Salem. Another was an orthodontist over in Seymour. If you had lived in southern Indiana any amount of time, an Apple had had his hands in your mouth and your pocketbook. Dentistry wasn't cheap.

Avonelle clutched her purse and gritted her teeth. "You take all cases?"

"Licensed, full-service." I pointed to Harry's high-priced paperwork on the wall.

Avonelle leaned forward. "Confidential?"

"Don't disclose our clients, unless required by subpoena." I wasn't totally sure if subpoena were the right word, but I reckoned mention of anything legal would impress Avonelle. Highfalutin people just love talking Latin. I hoped throwing out a foreign phrase or two would put Avonelle's mind at ease.

It did. She sucked in her gut and spilled the pork and beans. "It's about my husband, William."

"Isn't he deceased?"

"Year ago, this April."

"My condolences."

"Thank you. He lived a good life, but he left behind a few issues."

I could hear Veenie's little ears twitching. I knew she was hoping that William Apple had come back to haunt his wife.

202

Veenie loved a good ghost story. Her secret ambition in life was to be a ghost buster, and we'd just come off a hair-raising case chasing down ghosts and hillbilly hoodlums out at the old Wyatt mansion.

Avonelle pressed a hand over her mouth. Her blue eyes shone like cold ice chips. "He's dead, yes. But I've received some correspondence … and … it seems he left behind a few unresolved issues: three of them to be precise."

Avonelle unsnapped her purse. She pulled an envelope from her purse and a letter from that envelope. She unfolded the letter carefully and slid it across my desk.

The letter, handwritten, on stationary that featured mice in bonnets dancing in a chorus line along the top, was from one Ms. Barbara Skaggs. It appeared Doc Apple had spawned an illegitimate bushel of little apples. His self-proclaimed mistress, who lived in Hound Holler, had contacted Avonelle for child support. She had enclosed a snapshot of the fruit of William's loins, two boys and one girl. They were standing in height order in front of a picket fence. The fence was in need of a paint job. If you looked closely to the right, you could see a dog hightailing it out of the photo, just as it was snapped. It looked to be a beagle. The kids squinted into the camera, their tiny hands fisted at their sides.

"You responded to Ms. Skaggs?"

Avonelle twisted her lips. Clearly, she found that idea distasteful. "I was hoping the agency might do so on my behalf. Discretely. I had never heard of this young woman until this letter arrived. And well, hang it, of course I'd want proof that these children, any of them, belonged to my husband. I tend to doubt the whole accusation since Mr. Apple was never … well … never very experienced in that area."

Mrs. Apple stood. "You will need a retainer?"

"Five hundred will do her."

Mrs. Apple took out an embroidered clutch wallet. She retracted the exact amount in crisp one hundred dollar bills.

I handwrote her a receipt. "Give us a week," I said as I handed over the receipt.

Avonelle hesitated. "You will be discreet?"

I nodded.

Satisfied, Mrs. Apple headed toward the door. She hesitated as her hand touched the brass knob. She turned on her heel and said, her voice a little shaky, "You can tell Veenie she can come out from behind that file cabinet now." Without waiting for Veenie to show herself, Avonelle strutted out, head held high. She marched across the street toward the bank.

Veenie waited a few seconds before popping out from her hidey-hole. She strolled over and studied the photo of Barbara Skaggs's kids. "Not very experienced, eh? Well that don't look like the work of an amateur to me."

"Think those are his kids?"

Veenie slid off her glasses. She pushed the photo closer to her nose. "Hard to say, but this one," she pointed to the oldest, a towheaded boy who looked to be about ten years old, "has the Apple ears." The boy's ears flared out like tea cup handles. "This one too," said Veenie of the youngest, a girl of maybe four. "A shame. Girls with big ears don't outgrow them. She'll have to wear a shag all her life. That's what I'd do."

I had to agree about the ears. Most families had a defining feature. William's twin dentist sons, Bert and Bromley, were born with ears so generous they reminded one of wings. Avonelle, always mindful of looks, pinned her son's ears under hats on school picture days when they were younger. Things took an ugly turn when she found out the other kids had nicknamed her sons Dumbo One and Dumbo Two. In high school, she drove the boys to Indianapolis one weekend for some sort of secret surgery that tacked back their ears.

Veenie tapped the photo. "You ever hear of this Barbara Skaggs?"

"Knew some Skaggs over in Washington County. Hard to tell. Might be related." People in Pawpaw County weren't all that energetic. Most mated in county. It was like Genesis out here in corn country. Everybody begat everybody else. Made it harder to solve crimes because everybody's DNA was pretty much the same.

Veenie twitched her nose. "Wasn't there a Skaggs worked the acid ponds at the plastics factory with us?"

"Yep. Think his name was Lennie. But he died a few years back. Worked nights at Kelly's Paper Mill up in Brownstown. Got wasted long about 1989 on a Christmas bottle of Jim Beam. A one-ton roll of newsprint fell on him. He was nothing but a big grease spot in the end."

"If it's the Lennie Skaggs I'm thinking of, he didn't amount to much more than that when he was alive."

"Same Skaggs," I said.

I sat down at my desk, adjusted my glasses, and fired up the old computer. "Let's snoop on Barbara." I was born to power-drive a computer across the World Wild Web in search of facts. I would have made a humdinger of a Russian spy. It didn't take me but half an hour to gather a dossier on Ms. Barbara Skaggs. First off, Ms. Skaggs had never been married. Second, she seemed to live alone with the kids. All the bills—utilities, Internet, phone—were in her name. Last of all, she was employed as the head hostess at the Pancake Palace out on Highway 50.

Veenie read the pages on Barbara Skaggs as the printer spat them out. "Working at the Pancake Palace. Dealing with trade off Highway 50. That would make her more worldly than most. Probably where she met Doc Apple."

Everybody ate at the Pancake Palace. Sunday morning after church, if you were a Baptist. Wednesday nights after

Bible study, if you were a Lutheran. Just about any time if you were drunk or down in the dumps. Pancakes cheered everybody up.

"The Pancake Palace never closes," I said. "People go there all hours for the biscuits and gravy and the comfort food."

I eyed the photo of the Skaggs kids. It appeared Barbara Skaggs's womb might have been on the same 24/7/365 schedule as the Pancake Palace. It wasn't inconceivable that Doc Apple had enjoyed more than biscuits and gravy in his late-night quests for consolation. I reckoned anyone married to Avonelle might have needed a good bit of consoling over the years.

"Got a photo of Barbara?" Veenie asked.

I hit the print button. A photo slipped out of the printer. We studied the photo together.

Barbara wore square gunmetal glasses and squinted into the camera. Her forehead was creased in three places. Her hair was dark and dyed, with a wild flip above each ear. Her throat was long and skinny. It might also be described as scaly. She was wearing plastic daisy earrings, clip-ons from the looks of them. In the photo, she was wearing a flowered blouse with a rounded lace collar and a cardigan. She looked nothing like a Jezebel and more like a runaway Pentecost in need of a fashion intervention.

"Maybe she can cook?" suggested Veenie.

I shrugged. Not much of life looked like it did on TV. People loved to be big fish in small ponds. Knobby Waters was so small it was more like a mud puddle. It was not a town chock-full of beauty queens. Most people were pretty plain. Doc Apple had been more Don Knotts than Burt Reynolds. Still, I had no trouble seeing Barbara Skaggs and Will Apple lip-locked in a wanton embrace.

I glanced at my Timex. It was after five on Friday. Quitting time. I bundled up the paperwork on Barbara and stuck it in a file folder. I stuck the folder under my armpit, turned out the lights, and locked up.

Veenie and I ambled down the sidewalk to the Road Kill Café to see what was on the specials board for supper. Fridays, we always treated ourselves to a meal out. Halfway there I stopped thinking about Doc Apple and his biscuits and gravy ta-ta girl and began to wonder if the café would have any of Ma Horton's coconut cream pie. I hoped so, because I was planning on eating two pieces. All that talk about wanton sex had made me extra hungry.

Chapter Three

S aturday morning, assuming Barbara Skaggs would be home, we gassed up the '60 Impala and hot-footed it toward Hound Holler. The holler was a twenty-minute drive up the knobs, then down a gravel road that dropped deep into a butt-like crevice between two knobby hills.

In Knobby Waters, there were two kinds of people: town people or holler people. Everyone knew which they were, which they aspired to be, and which they hoped to God never to become. Barbara Skaggs was not among the fortunate. She lived smack on Hound Holler Road. One look at her rented house and you knew she'd given up all hope, along with a good bit of her self-respect, about a decade ago.

The plan was to stake out Barbara's place, see if anything untoward might be going on that would lead her to engage in unscrupulous acts to earn a little egg money on the side. Barbara lived in To Jo Scott's old farmhouse, which had been nice enough back in the day, meaning the Depression. These days, the house looked more like something out of Mother Goose. The roof was a mossy carpet. Foot-tall maple saplings sprouted from the gutters. The front porch, which was missing most of its spindle posts, sagged in a toothless grin. A sway-backed barn struggled to remain erect in the backyard. A scarecrow made of moldy corn stalks, wearing a tattered, brown-felt hat and a large overall jacket with patches, stood watch over rows of corn stubble and what may have once been tomato vines.

I had a pair of binoculars resting on the bridge of my nose. My glasses were off, laid on the seat of the Impala between me and Veenie. A family-sized bag of pork rinds we'd picked up at the Go Go Gas rested on the seat between us. It was almost noon. We were on stakeout behind a tall stand of weeds in a tractor pull-off on the soft shoulder of Hound Holler creek. We were just across from Barbara Skaggs's place.

Barbara's oldest boy, the one with the pitcher ears, was playing with a rusty dump truck along a line of mud puddles in the front yard. He was chasing a rooster back and forth. The rooster, all wings, was squawking, occasionally trying to peck the dump truck to death. Every now and then, another boy, dressed only in ragged denim shorts, the nipples of his bare chest blue as raisins, would burst around the corner of the house trying to lasso a chicken. He was wearing a red cowboy hat and shooting a cap gun.

Veenie asked, "You gonna eat them pork rinds?"

"Nah. Have at 'em."

For the next ten minutes, while I watched the boys trying to lasso chickens, Veenie crunched pig skin. Stakeouts had never been portrayed like this back when I was watching *Magnum, PI*. I tried to shut my ears as Veenie crunched pig skins, then washed it all down with a quart of chocolate milk. She topped off the skins with a fistful of fruit-flavored Tums. Why that woman suffered from perpetual heartburn was no mystery to me.

It was a May day and had rained all night. It was getting steamy in the Impala. I punched out the wing on the window to let more air circulate and motioned for Veenie to do the same.

Veenie had been fidgety all morning. She wore stretch capri pants. It was approaching noon, and the white leather and plastic seats on the Impala were heating up. Her plump little calves were sticking to the seats. She licked the last of the pork rind salt from her fingertips and belched.

I said, "Dr. Duhaney," that was Veenie's cardiologist, "wouldn't approve of you eating all that salt and fat."

"Dr. Doohickey can go suck an egg."

Veenie made a show of fanning herself with a fluorescent sales circular for chicken parts from the Hoosier Feedbag. She was growing impatient. "Let's bust on in."

I drew the binoculars away from my eyes and slipped on my glasses. "You want to do the questioning?"

"Nah. I want to be the muscle."

We never carried firearms—left that to Harry, who ran the collections department—but Veenie's BB pistol was in the glove compartment. The toy pistol looked real. It was the expensive model, with a solid wood handle and brass trimming. It shot BB pellets. Men tended to wet themselves when they saw two nearsighted old ladies packing a piece. The criminals we dealt with were the world's biggest pantywaists. Most of them surrendered as soon as Veenie waved the pistol. They fell to their knees and blubbered like babies. Veenie enjoyed cuffing them. The Shades Agency used those new-fangled, plastic twist-tie cuffs. Bringing a perp down was a lot like bagging the kitchen trash: very satisfying to any woman who'd wasted her youth as a frustrated housewife.

Bored with waiting, we scrambled out of the Impala and walked across the muddy road to the farmhouse. The oldest boy stared us down. "You Holy Rollers?"

I tried to look sweet, harmless. "We're looking for your Mama, Barbara Skaggs? She home?"

The boy hiked up his shorts and circled me, then Veenie. He brushed a flap of dirty blond hair out of his eyes. His ears were big enough to catch and hold rainwater. "You bill collectors?"

Veenie eyed the boy. "We look like bill collectors?"

The boy wiped his nose on the back of his hand. "Nah, you look like old ladies."

They were standing at the porch now. The boy asked Veenie, "That a real gun?"

"Sure." She pointed the pistol right at his head.

The boy screamed, "Mama!" and ran into the house. The torn screen door banged after him.

A squinting woman wearing gunmetal glasses appeared in the doorway. A child appeared in the doorway next to her. It was the girl with the big ears. She clung to the balloon legs of her mother's baggy shorts. One watery blue eye peeked out trying to get a good look at us without exposing herself.

"Don't want any," Barbara said.

I slid my big foot into the doorway. "Mrs. William Apple sent us."

Barbara opened the door wide and stepped back. She bent and picked up the little girl, lifting her up until she could ride down on her hip. "Well, come on in, then. Been expecting someone."

Once we were inside, Barbara seemed welcoming, not at all unreasonable. "I want what's due the children. Child support, you know," she explained.

I nodded sympathetically. "You have proof? Mrs. Apple would need proof before money could change hands."

Barbara pressed her knuckles to her lips and mulled over the question. "What would I need?"

"DNA. Tests cost a hundred dollars each. You'd have to deposit that with us."

Barbara looked at her two younger children. They were tumbling over each other like dung beetles on the braided rug in front of the TV. The TV was on, but Barbara had clicked down the sound when we took our seats in the living room.

"Can't we just test one of them? Assume the others would be the same? I work at the Pancake Palace. Don't make a heap of money. I mean, if I had money to throw around, I wouldn't be writing to Mrs. Apple now, would I? But William up and died.

He used to give me an allowance. And that was fine. But now Billy Junior there," she pointed to the oldest boy, "needs braces. William's cousin was supposed to take care of that. Wasn't supposed to cost me a dime. Show the nice ladies, Billy."

Billy Junior pulled back his gums, revealing a gap between his two front teeth. It was identical to the gap Avonelle's boys had sported at about the same age before their cousin the orthodontist had intervened.

I considered the options. "Maybe we could test the oldest boy. Make a good faith gesture. You could save up. Do the others one at a time."

"You mean like layaway?" The creases eased in Barbara's forehead. "I don't mean her no harm." She bit her lip. She gathered the collar of her cardigan closer to her throat. "I knew William was married, but he seemed sweet. And he was lonely. Guess I was too."

I could tell Barbara wanted to talk about it, but I didn't want to hear the Jerry Springer version of the whole sordid affair. Every time people talked about sex, I got hungry. My butt couldn't afford the extra pounds.

Veenie came to my rescue. "I can run out. Get a spit kit from the Chevy."

"Won't take but a minute," I promised. "If Billy Junior would oblige us, we could be on our way. Takes a week to get the test back. We could discuss confidential payment possibilities and arrangements with Avonelle in the meantime."

Barbara stood and smoothed the front of her shorts. She eyed Billy Junior, who was rolling around on the rug on his back with all fours in the air panting like a dying dog. "All he has to do is spit? No written tests?"

"Yep, just spit in a tube."

"Well, I reckon he can do that all right."

Veenie was out the door. But almost as soon as the front screen door slammed, she was screeching at me. "Ruby Jane? Uh, can you come out here for a second. We got us a little, uh, problem."

I ambled toward the door and peered out onto the porch. A man was slumped in the metal porch glider. He was wearing the tattered brown hat and denim overcoat that the barn scarecrow had been wearing when we had first arrived. At first I thought someone had dragged the scarecrow onto the porch. But on closer inspection, I could see that it wasn't a scarecrow but one of Avonelle's sons, one of the Apple twins, Bert or Bromley, I couldn't tell which. They weren't identical twins, but they were close.

His mouth was open. He could have been snoring. But from the cool white of his face—it looked like a peeled egg—and the way his body slumped, not a tense muscle in him, I could tell he was toast. A speckled chicken was perched on the glider rest next to him, pecking at his lifeless hand.

I looked at Veenie.

She shrugged. "Don't look at me. He wasn't sitting there when we went in."

Barbara stepped out on the porch and stood next to Veenie. She looked a little green, like a thinly sliced zucchini. She hugged herself. "I don't know a darn thing about that," she said, sounding defensive.

END BOOK 2 EXCERPT

Don't miss any of Ruby Jane and Veenie's crime-cracking capers.

Order your copy of the *Baby Daddy Mystery, The Shady Hoosier Detective Series: Book 2,* today at Daisy's Website: https://www.daisypettles.com

Acknowledgments

Many thanks to all the great friends who read drafts of the *Ghost Busting Mystery* and provided invaluable feedback that helped me create the world of Knobby Waters and its quirky characters.

A special shout-out goes to my Jackson and Lawrence County Hoosier Facebook friends, whose stories and daily postings helped spark the creation of this series.

This book would not have been possible without my mother, Reva June Phillips, of Bedford, Indiana, who fed me books of every kind from as far back as I can remember, and her mother, Anabelle England, of Brownstown, Indiana, who did the same. I was born into a house of books and read to until my ears burned and my imagination soared. Lucky me. Growing up in a small town in southern Indiana, I had the great good fortune of attending a tiny school where everybody knew my name and where the rules of the English language were taken seriously and instilled in all students whether we cared to learn them or not. (Thank you, Wilma Scharbrough).

I have to thank the Burlington Writer's Workshop (BWW). Vermont is my adopted home state, and the folks at the BWW were very generous in sharing their ideas for improving this book. I am especially grateful to Diane Donovan, Robin Zabiegalski, and Laney Webber for their suggestions for improving the work overall. This series was inspired by the swapping of porch stories between me and my great friend, Linda Beal, one summer when I was in horrible, desperate need of a laugh or two. Linda helped me tap into long-lost memories of Kentuckiana and its good-hearted people. Way to go Sneeter. I can never thank you enough.

The town of Knobby Waters is not a real place, nor is there a Pawpaw County anywhere in the great state of Indiana. I did, however, grow up in Medora, Indiana, a tiny river town in Jackson County. Those who live around Jackson, Washington, Lawrence, Pike, and Orange County, Indiana may recognize in these books a host of half-forgotten, tiny towns, many of which still pepper the hilly (some say knobby) landscape in the southern part of the state.

Southern Indiana is, in many ways, more a part of the South than the North. The southern Indiana dialect, known as the South Midland Dialect, infuses the speech of this region with a peculiar drawl, and that drawl along with the dropping and stretching of many vowels, colors the speech of the farmers and families who populate this area. The aphorisms in this book are true to the region, many of them borrowed from conversations with my mother and my big sisters, Ginger East, of Bedford, Indiana, and Cathy Smith, of Medora, Indiana, and my little sister, Tammy McPike, of Greasy Creek, Indiana.

I have, from time to time, borrowed the surnames that surrounded me as a child in an effort to lend authenticity to the book, and as a playful way to bring back to life many of the small-town characters I knew growing up. I really did, for example, have an Uncle Dode, though he has long since passed and bore no resemblance to the character of the same name in this series. My great friends Melissa and Pete Horton of Mitchell, Indiana, who always make me laugh, really do raise chickens (They'd have a Chickenlandia, if they could.). They were kind enough to name a chicken after me. Unfortunately, she went too free with her range and was recently eaten by a mangy possum.

While I freely borrow Hoosier surnames, any similarities between real people and the characters of Knobby Waters are coincidental, not meant to capture the essence of any living person or family. Like most writers, I have sewn together tiny scraps of reality and fragments of a half-remembered childhood into a tent of tall tales whose sole purpose is to delight and entertain.

Pretty much everything in the *Shady Hoosier Detective Agency Series* is fanciful storytelling. May you enjoy reading these books as much as I enjoyed writing them, and may you spend many a pleasant hour eating pie, fishing for catfish in Greasy Creek, and hanging out on porch swings with the zany citizens of Knobby Waters, Indiana.

Visit me online anytime at https://www.daisypettles.com.

Subscribe there to the Knobby Waters newsletter to receive free gifts, T-shirts, and advance notice of forthcoming books. I'll be publishing the latest gossip from Knobby Waters and introducing you to new characters as they push their way into consciousness and print.

Keep in touch and. I promise I'll do likewise.

About the Author

Daisy Pettles is the pen name of Vicky Phillips, born in Bedford, Indiana. She grew up in Medora, Indiana, where her parents ran the gas station and ice cream stand. She learned to read while sitting on her grandmother's lap, under an apple tree in Brownstown, Indiana. As a child, she was fed a steady diet of books, pies, and Bible stories. Her favorite song was "I'll Be a Sunbeam for Jesus." Graduating Medora High School in 1977, she attended DePauw University, where she was graduated Phi Beta Kappa. A world traveler, she has lived in San Francisco, London, and Athens. She has raced camels in Egypt and eaten Kentucky Fried Chicken with Communists in Shanghai. She was a therapist before becoming an Internet entrepreneur, designing America's first online university system in 1989. Her current home lays at the end of a dirt road in Vermont. For all her travels, her heart remains a Hoosier. She loves persimmon pudding and stories where good stomps all over evil. *The Shady Hoosier Detective Series*, a comic crime cozy set in the fictitious Knobby Waters, Indiana, is her debut mystery novel series.

Blog Website: https://www.daisypettles.com

Email: daisy@daisypettles.com

Twitter: @DaisyPettles

Facebook: https://www.facebook.com/daisy.pettles.author

Made in the USA
Middletown, DE
22 February 2023

25379451R00126